JUNGLE TALES

Airship 27 Productions

Jungle Tales-Volume 1
"The Path of Life & Death" © 2012 Aaron Smith
"The Devil's Nest" © 2012 Duane Spurlock
"Ki-Gor & the Secret of the Vikings" © 2012 W. Peter Miller

Published by Airship 27 Productions
www.airship27.com
www.airship27hangar.com

Interior llustrations © 2012 Kelly Everaert
Cover illustration © 2012 Bryon Fowler

Editor: Ron Fortier
Associate Editor: Charles Saunders
Production and design: Rob Davis.

ISBN-13 978-0615659978
ISBN-10:0615659977

Printed in the United States of America

10 9 8 7 6 5 4 3 2 1

JUNGLE TALES
Volume One
(FEATURING KI-GOR, LORD OF THE JUNGLE)

THE PATH OF LIFE & DEATH

To save a benevolent jungle queen, Ki-Gor must battle a village of cannibals and a crazed witch doctor.

THE DEVIL'S NEST

The search for a lost heir to an American fortune sends Ki-Gor into an unexplored part of the jungle where an ancient terror lurks.

KI-GOR & THE SECRET OF THE VIKINGS

Deep inside a hidden jungle valley, Ki-Gor stumbles on a colony of Norsemen with a giant berserker as their leader.

THE ALLURE OF THE JUNGLE

The Path of Life and Death

By Aaron Smith

The large warthog lumbered slowly among the tall grass of the plains. It was a big one, five feet long and almost 330 pounds. His big snout concentrated its sniffing on the ground as he searched for something to satisfy his hunger. Warthogs are omnivorous and will eat almost anything; certain grasses, mushrooms, small dead animals, roots, berries, bark, and the eggs of many birds. Their vision is poor, but is more than compensated for by their superb sense of smell, which is the primary means by which a warthog finds its food.

Unfortunately for the old, fat warthog, he never did find his breakfast. Death came swiftly, as a blur of golden fur and flashing fangs exploded onto the scene. A chaos of gold and brown and red erupted and the lightning fast lion took down his prey. The warthog, who had been hungry a moment before, now quenched the merciless hunger of the African lion, who fed ravenously, leaving behind only a lifeless wreckage of bone and tusk, left to dry in the hot sub-Saharan sun.

From his hidden perch in a tall tree nearby, Ki-Gor had witnessed the entire deadly drama. He had intentionally remained silent, giving neither the warthog nor the lion any indication that he was near. He didn't want to interfere, but simply wished to watch. He marveled, as he always did, at the speed and ferocity of the lion on the hunt. There was no malice as the lion took down his victim, Ki-Gor knew. The lion was simply doing what nature had given it to do. He was watching the order of things as they were meant to be, and he had the utmost appreciation for the spectacle.

Unlike the lion and the warthog, Ki-Gor was not typical of the natural inhabitants of the African continent. He had been christened as Robert Kilgour, the son of a Scottish missionary who had come to Africa to spread the word of his religion among the native peoples of this dark and dangerous continent. His father had died in the jungle, leaving the poor son behind to fend for himself. He had managed to survive and to thrive even, alone and unsupervised. Now a man, he called himself Ki-Gor, a variation on the family name he had been born with. He was at home here in Africa, and he would have chosen no other place in the world to live if he had the option to do so.

Ki-Gor was six feet tall, powerfully muscled, with blue eyes that had an undertone of grey to them. His hair was long, cut only rarely, when it grew long enough to interfere with his movements through the trees and along the rivers and fields of the wild parts of this land. It was the lightest of blonde hair, bleached by the sun to an almost white shade. His skin had been toughened by the rugged life he lived in the jungles, and was bronzed to a deep golden color by the same burning sun that had lightened his hair.

As he looked down upon the feasting lion, he thought of his place here among the citizens of the jungle, and he was happy. Ki-Gor was not a complete stranger to the ways of what those from elsewhere considered civilization. He had been to their cities and towns and had seen the things they did to amuse themselves. He knew that they liked to sit in darkened rooms and watch moving pictures of people acting out stories on screens lit by electric light, but he found no appeal in these gaudy artificial images. In Ki-Gor's mind, there was simply no comparison between these things and the real beauty, savage though it might be, of the jungles and plains of Africa. Why any man would choose to live in the falsified confines of a city was beyond his understanding. He much preferred the openness of vast blue skies, the true light of the sun, the twinkling of innumerable stars overhead at night, and the freely blowing breezes of the high-grassed vistas of his adopted homeland. This was Ki-Gor's land.

Not terribly far from where Ki-Gor watched the drama of the lion and the warthog was the village of Jorowan. It was a medium sized native village with a fairly sizable population of men, who hunted and gathered the food that kept the people fed, and of women who cooked the food the men brought home and cared for the children who would one day grow up to hunt and gather and cook for themselves. The people of Jorowan led a simple and mostly peaceful existence. There was an occasional battle, a savage clash with those people of neighboring villages who would sometimes come in a raid to try to seize territory or goods, but these little wars were few and far between. For most of the time, life went on in the village as it had for many years, perhaps even centuries.

Jorowan was composed of an arrangement of many huts sitting in clumps in a large circular clearing in the thick of the jungle. For several miles around the village, tangles of tall trees, branches, vines, and underbrush made the area treacherous and confusing to any one not used to navigating their way through such dense foliage. As one approached the village, they would find that the thickness suddenly stops, giving way to the spacious area wherein the village was built up. Between and around the huts, men and women walked and worked, children played, and life went on as it usually did in villages like Jorowan. One hut sat in the northernmost corner of the village, slightly further from its neighbors than the other huts. This was one of the larger huts, and was notable for the weird arcane items that decorated the space just above and outside the door. Roots and herbs hung in strange arrangements. Animal bones were hung in bizarre patterns. One human skull served as the centerpiece of this morbid series of talismans and charms. Theses things, as anyone familiar with the customs of such jungle tribes would know, signified that within this hut dwelt a shaman or sorceress. There was one of these mysterious religious leaders in every village, for the people depended on them not only for spiritual guidance, but for healing as well. However, on this day the local magic dealer was not the one doing the healing, but was the one in dire need of help.

The man called Luther had been called to come to this particular hut. Within the hut dwelt the village priestess, A'Laka. She was still young, but skilled in the magic of the jungle, and her reputation as a sorceress and healer had earned her great respect among the people of Jorowan. Luther was her only true confidant. He came whenever she called, and aided her in her duties whenever she asked. On this day, she had sent a messenger to tell him to come at once to her hut. By the tone of the messenger's voice and the expression upon his face, Luther had sensed that it was a matter of urgency, and he had ceased what he had been doing and come as quickly as he was able. Now, he entered the hut, concern showing in the deep creases in the dark skin of his face.

Luther was something of an oddity among the natives of this village and others like it; he was a fat man. It was not as though the others in his village were starving, but life was not easy in the jungle and the people toiled in the hot sun, burning away most excess weight. Therefore, it was unusual to see a man as large as Luther walking among the people of Jorowan. He was tall too and, with his thick frame and round bald head, could be an intimidating figure. This dramatic appearance gave him a fitting look for the aide to a village priestess, who herself had to be a figure of mysterious habits and exotic beauty in order to be effective in her role.

Luther entered the hut. The openings on the side, primitive versions of windows, were covered by strips of dried grass in order to shut out most of the daylight. A single candle burned in the center of the room, bathing the interior in a pale light. The village priestess was reclining on her bed of thick lion fur blankets. She was young, in her twenties, a light-skinned black woman of breathtaking beauty. Normally, the sight of her was enough to boil the blood of even a stern older man like Luther, but today she looked weak and sickly. Luther, unaccustomed to seeing A'Laka in such a state, was immediately filled with concern.

"My priestess, are you unwell?" he asked with sincere worry behind his words, "the messenger summoned me with great urgency, and I sensed that something was amiss."

A'Laka looked up at the man who had helped her so many times in the past. "I must leave this place at once, Luther," she said, as she began to rise from her seated position. She tried to stand, but swayed weakly and fell back upon the bed.

"You, my priestess, are in no condition to go anywhere! What is it?" asked the concerned man.

A'Laka sighed and continued to speak, "It was a dream, old friend, but a dream that was more than a dream! My sister, far away from here in her own village, lies dying! She has fallen ill. I must go to her! Only the healing powers that we share as twins and priestesses can save her. I must go to her!"

Luther's face turned into a stone cold mask of dead serious worry. "You cannot even stand on your feet! Such a journey would kill you. I have never understood the workings of your strange powers, but it is clear to me that if your sister is ill, so must you be. I have never before seen you so drained of life, of vitality! You must not even try to travel. Even were you strong now, the jungle holds too many perils and you must not take such a risk. The people of Jorowan need you!"

A'Laka managed to stand. She had to exert all her energy to do so, and the strain was visible on her face. She spoke back to Luther, "I know the journey will be long and perilous. A great portion of the continent lies between her village and mine, but consider this, Luther; if one of us should die, the power of the other will be cut in half at first, and then slowly fade away with all our strength, and then our very life! My life and her life are bound together by blood! There must be a way...there must..."

She had excited herself to such a degree that her weakened legs could no longer support her, and she fell back onto the bed of thick lion skins.

"Rest, priestess," begged Luther. "You cannot make such a journey. Rest and perhaps you can find another way to aid your sister."

At Luther's words, the young priestess seemed to summon a second wind, and she sat straight up. "Yes, Luther! Another way! But who; who will be the one? Who can we trust with so vital a task?"

Luther looked confused. He wasn't quite sure what A'Laka was talking about. He watched as she stood up and walked across the floor of the hut. She seemed to have regained some of her strength and indeed was no longer on the verge of collapse. She went over to where the implements of her sorcerous arts were kept. Luther watched with fascination as she looked through her things, her eyes glazed and trance-like as she searched for the proper tools. She picked up a small clay pot with a lid. She opened it and placed it on the small wooden table in front of which she often knelt when preparing her healing potions. She sat cross-legged by the small table. Then she produced a sharp dagger and proceeded to run it across the palm of her hand, slicing into her flesh.

Luther reacted in horror to the sight of her wounding herself. "What are you doing?" he bellowed.

She held her hand over the small clay pot, letting her blood drip into the container as she replied to Luther, "I'm finding another way. You forbid me to go to her, so I shall send a part of me. I will touch her from many miles away. By our bond of blood I shall save her!"

She placed the cover on the small vessel and then tied a strip of cloth around her hand to stop the bleeding. The wound had looked more serious than it actually had been and was already beginning to clot. Luther suspected that the dagger's blade may have been treated with some sort of healing herb. He did not know enough of A'Laka's magic to know if he was correct, but he considered it a valid possibility.

She held the clay container up and spoke to him again, "Now who will bring this to her? You asked me to find another way, Luther. I give you one. Now you must decide how this may travel south, down, down to the faraway village of my sister, to accomplish its vital task!"

Luther laughed out loud. It was not a mocking laughter, but an outburst of appreciation for the talents of the priestess, talents that always amazed him. "You wish me to find a messenger? Some fool who will travel all those miles with a little pot of blood?"

A'Laka waved an outstretched finger over the top of the container. Luther could swear that he saw sparks, strange glowing spots of light dancing over it with her gesture. Then she pointed straight at him. "Go, Luther! Time is all important now. Go!"

Luther turned and exited the hut. When he was gone, the priestess released the iron-willed discipline that had kept her standing. She fell upon her bed, and sleep overtook her as easily as a cheetah outruns a sloth.

Luther walked around the village for awhile, pondering what to do next. The health and well-being of the priestess was foremost on his mind. The people of this village depended on her, not only for her healing powers, but for her ability to protect the people from the dark things of the jungle; the evil spirits and hostile magicians. As far as Luther was concerned, A'Laka was the glue that held the village together, as vital as the mightiest hunter or the wisest elder. If her life was indeed in danger because of her connection to her ailing sister, then it was Luther's obligation to his people to find a way to help them both. He wondered how he would get that strange little pot of her blood to her sister, so many miles away through such treacherous terrain. Were he still a young man, Luther would have braved the many dangers of the journey and taken it there himself. But Luther's youth was a thing of the past. He had gained much wisdom, but had lost his old speed and strength. The jungle would have no mercy on him at his age. He could not go. He thought of the various men who made up the population of his village. There were many strong warriors, young men who could run with great speed, experienced hunters who had faced lions and snakes and charging rhinos. Still, he could not think of any among them who possessed the raw courage and discipline that would be needed to make such a long and dangerous trek along the length of the continent. Were he to ask for volunteers, many would step forward. Of this he was certain, but he did not think any of them would survive the journey's perils long enough to deliver the elixir to the priestess's twin. Who could he trust? Who could survive such an ordeal? One name came to his worried mind, and that name was Ki-Gor.

The "jungle grapevine," as some called it, was the means by which some of the tribes in that area of Africa communicated. Several groups of natives had an alliance of sorts. There were no hostilities among these tribes and they sometimes cooperated for the good of all. Drumming had long been a way of sending messages in the jungle, and this small group of tribes had devised a method of sending these messages to each other. Each village was equipped with several large drums. When a message had to be sent from one village to another, the drums were utilized. The drummer in the first village would pound out his message, in a sort of rhythmic code, until the nearest village replied by way of drumming, and then sent the message on to the next stop along the grapevine. So on went the message, drummed out carefully, until it reached the village for which it was meant. On this particular day, Luther gave instructions to the village drummer of Jorowan. The drummer began to beat on his instrument, sending out the sound that could be translated by any who knew the code. The next village picked up the beat and the drumming continued, carrying Luther's words across vast distances until it reached its destination.

In the village of the Kamozila pygmies, Chief N'Geeso perked up his ears as he heard the drumming sounds coming from the next village. Mentally, he interpreted the carefully timed drumbeats. He understood the message, "Please summon Ki-Gor. Luther of Jorowan wishes to see him. It is a matter of life or death."

N'Geeso instructed his drummer to reply that the message had been receieved and understood. Once this was done, the four foot tall warrior chief grabbed his spear and ran off into the jungle to deliver the message to a certain place where the sounds of the drums could not penetrate.

Miles from the pygmy village, deep in the jungle, where the trees and brush were thickest and men rarely travelled, was an impressively designed set of platforms, held up and interconnected by about a dozen trees. This was the place where Ki-Gor often dwelled. While his official home was located on a plantation on the eastern edge of the Congo, he felt much more at home deep in the jungle. This house among the trees was where he went when he had the desire to retreat from civilization. He and his American-born wife, Helene, had arrived here a few days earlier, happy to have the chance to spend some time alone together. Ki-Gor stood on the topmost level of the tree house, looking out over the tree tops, breathing in the lush moist air of the jungle afternoon. From several levels below, the scent of cooking meat drifted upward to where Ki-Gor stood. Helene was cooking lunch. The aroma made him salivate and he prepared to swing downward on the vines to claim his share of the food. Just as he was about to begin his descent, he paused. In the thick of the jungle, about one hundred meters away, his sharp eyes had noticed a glimmer, a spot of light reflected off steel. The presence of steel meant the presence of man!

Instead of climbing downward towards Helene and his lunch, Ki-Gor grabbed hold of one of the nearby vines and swung himself outward, leaping from tree to tree, moving swiftly but quietly towards the source of the reflection. As he drew closer, he could tell from the sound of footsteps that only one person was approaching. This should be no great threat, Ki-Gor told himself. He leaped into the open, planning his movements to bring him face to face with whoever was there. As he revealed himself, he recognized his target. It was N'Geeso! Ki-Gor burst out laughing. "Old friend, you were nearly greeted by the point of my dagger!" he joked. "Announce yourself next time!"

N'Geeso joined his friend in the short burst of laughter, and the two walked together back to the tree house. The three of them, Ki-Gor, his wife, and his friend, ate together and N'Geeso told of the drum-beaten summons. Ki-Gor asked N'Geeso to escort Helene back to the plantation. He would have trusted his own life to the pygmy, so he would place the life of his wife in his hands without hesitation. Though short of stature, N'Geeso was a fierce and able warrior. N'Geeso and Helene departed in one direction and Ki-Gor went in the other, towards Jorowan. He would go to find out what Luther thought was so important.

Having spent most of his life in the jungles of Africa, and being especially familiar with this area, Ki-Gor knew the best routes of travel from one village to another. He was aware of just where the rivers narrowed to make crossing them easier. He knew what areas held dangers which were best avoided by going around them. He knew where the most well-worn paths were and he knew how to use the rising and falling sides and crests of the hills to make any trip go by faster and more easily. This was Ki-Gor's land, his home, and he knew it well. He respected the jungle, and in return it showed him all its secrets. He made it to Jorowan faster than anyone who did not know him could have anticipated.

Ki-Gor strode into Jorowan in the late afternoon. As usual, he travelled light, wearing only his leopard skin loincloth and the belt that held his knife and a small leather pouch which was empty at the moment, but was always there, since it had come in handy many times before. On his back was his powerful bow, with which he was an expert marksman, and a quiver of arrows. Those few things were all Ki-Gor needed. Anything else he desired, the jungle would provide.

As he entered the small village, he was greeted by many of the natives. Ki-Gor was well known and loved by the peaceful villagers of the area. It would be hard to find a tribe that had not been helped by Ki-Gor in some way over the span of years in which he had lived in this area. He smiled and greeted some of the children as they came running over to talk to him. He got down on one knee and spoke with them for a few minutes, until a long, wide shadow was cast over him. He looked up and saw that the shadow's source was Luther. He got up and shook the hand of the man who had called him to Jorowan with such urgency as had sent N'Geeso to find him right away.

Luther greeted Ki-Gor in a friendly manner, but the jungle lord could see a deep feeling of worry written on the villager's face. Before Ki-Gor had a chance to ask what was the matter, Luther motioned for him to follow. They walked across the village, passing many people, but the villagers could tell by the way he walked with Luther that Ki-Gor was here on a matter of business, and they disturbed him no more. The two men reached the front of A'Laka's hut and Luther led Ki-Gor inside.

A'Laka was reclining on her fur-covered bed when they entered. She looked weak, but even in her current state of illness was still ravishingly beautiful. She managed to smile as she saw who had entered.

"Luther, you have brought the great pale prince of the jungle himself to see me," she said. "Illness has certain advantages then. How are you, old friend?"

Ki-Gor detected the hint of sarcasm behind her words. Several years earlier, before he had met and married Helene Vaughn, Ki-Gor had had a brief romance with A'Laka. To him, it had only been a short, but passionate, dalliance. He had never intended for it to be anything else. A'Laka had had other ideas. She had wished to permanently possess Ki-Gor, and had even resorted to trying some jungle magic on him when he tried to break away from the relationship. His iron will had allowed him to resist her charms and the affair had ended. Apparently, thought Ki-Gor, she still held a little hostility over those events. He held no grudge towards her, since no permanent harm had been done, except perhaps to her pride. He could tell immediately that she was not well, and his concern for her overwhelmed any unpleasant memories from the past.

A'Laka motioned for Luther and Ki-Gor to sit. They did so and the young priestess proceeded to tell Ki-Gor what Luther already knew; of her illness and how she knew it to be caused by her sister's even more dire condition, of the potion she had prepared to heal them both, which now consisted of not only her blood but also various herbs and roots found in the nearby jungle, and of how she needed someone to traverse the dangerous lands between Jorowan and its sister village to the south.

Ki-Gor, as Luther had known he would, immediately volunteered to make the journey himself. Ki-Gor was a generous man and was always ready to take a chance to save a life, or two in this case. Once he had accepted the task, A'Laka began to explain certain specific details which

A'Laka…was still ravishingly beautiful.

would make the mission much more treacherous.

"You must understand, Ki-Gor, that the magic of my tribe is tied to our history in a very exact way. If you are to carry out this quest and succeed, it must be done in a certain way. The mixture of medicines that you must bring to my sister will lose its potency if you leave the trail that was taken when a number of our people in her village left there to migrate here, to my village. It is a path through dangerous regions, and only the strongest of men can traverse it and live! Luther, find a map!"

Luther, always anticipating the priestess's needs, produced a rolled up parchment from his belt. He unfurled it and laid it flat on the small table in the hut. It was a crude, but understandable, representation of the entire portion of the continent in which they now sat. The village of Jorowan was clearly marked on the map, as was its sister village, which was called Tapara. Jorowan was at the top or northern section of the map, and Tapara was fairly far to the south. From one of the twin villages to the other was a long, occasionally winding trail. Luther's chubby finger traced the trail along the map as Ki-Gor and A'Laka watched.

"This is the way you must travel," explained the sorceress's aide. "Only by this route may the potion be carried and retain its powers of healing."

"I see," said Ki-Gor, his face showing no emotion, but his heart knowing what dangers lay along that route, for it would take him straight through an area known as The Forest of Dusk.

The Forest of Dusk, Ki-Gor was fully aware, was a section of jungle where the trees grew so tall and thick that it perpetually had the appearance of twilight, even at the height of noon. Because the lack of light made it so difficult to see one's surroundings clearly, danger could sneak up easily, often with deadly results. This was made more perilous by the fact that the natives of this area were known to be fierce and unrelenting cannibals. Few men would have the raw nerve required to undertake a journey through that terrible region for any reason. Many a traveler had entered The Forest of Dusk and was never seen or heard from again. That part of the journey made even the courageous Ki-Gor a bit nervous. Looking at the map some more, he knew that it also would take him through other dangerous areas, but he would leave thoughts of those places until after he had made his way through that dark and cannibal-infested region. That place, and his attempts to pass through it alive would be his most immediate concern.

While looking at the map, he mentally calculated the time it would take him to make the trip. "Going at my best speed, and stopping only to rest for a few hours, it should take me about three days to reach Tapara," he told

Luther and A'Laka, "I will leave at the first light of the morning."

Luther brought some food and Ki-Gor and A'Laka ate. Then Ki-Gor slept through the night on a spare skin in Luther's hut. As the sun rose, so did the jungle lord. He placed the small clay pot containing A'Laka's healing concoction in the pouch that hung from his belt. Then he left Jorowan and began his trek into the wild lands between the two villages. His mission of mercy had begun.

Ki-Gor's physical condition was at the very peak of what was possible for a human being. Raising himself in the jungle and surviving countless hardships had honed his body to near perfection. He was incredibly strong, amazingly fast, and tougher than almost any man he had ever encountered. He used no horse or other transportation to make his way through the jungle; only his strength, speed, stamina, and willpower, all helped by his encyclopedic knowledge of the land and its inhabitants; human, animal, and plant. The first few hours of the journey were easy ones. It was a clear, warm morning and the trip started on even terrain in sparsely covered ground. Ki-Gor was able to maintain his top speed for long stretches at a time and his pace for the first day's travel was quite good. He stopped briefly around noon to eat some berries and take a drink from a crisp, clear stream.

Morning gave way to afternoon and Ki-Gor kept moving. He had covered many miles when the jungle brush began to grow thicker the further he went. It slowed him slightly, but he was still able to keep up an impressive pace, leaping over small obstacles and running on. Little by little, the trees seemed to be closer together, the underbrush grew more and more dense, and the leaves, branches and vines overhead began to dampen the amount of sunlight that was permitted to penetrate the jungle. Ki-Gor's sharp vision did an adequate enough job of compensating for the gathering darkness at first, but sooner than he had anticipated, the darkness was far deeper than it should have been at this point in the day. Ki-Gor knew that he had come to the beginning of the Forest of Dusk. He made a concentrated effort to keep his sharp senses even more on alert than usual. He knew that the deadliest of dangers could be lurking around any corner, behind any tree, and about to strike from any direction.

Ki-Gor's instincts, as well as his senses, had been honed to razor-sharpness by so many years of jungle life. This had led to his developing a sort of intuition, which could be said to be a combination of sensory skill and wisdom gained from experience. There in the darkness of the Forest of

Dusk, the mighty jungle lord's intuition told him that danger had finally drawn near. He sensed that he was no longer the only human being in the area. Whoever was near, he told himself, was skilled at sneaking through the trees and knew the area well, for he could not tell how many there were, or exactly where they were. He just knew he had visitors. He stopped in his tracks, his ears straining to detect any hint of movement. For half a minute there was nothing…and then all hell broke loose! There was a horrifically mad shrieking sound and suddenly a man leaped from the branches of the trees and landed standing directly in front of Ki-Gor! He was a tall but wiry black man, with his face painted in bright hues of red and yellow. He was naked and wielded a machete. He shrieked and bellowed in tones that were obviously meant to sound inhuman and animal-like. His intention could have been nothing less than to frighten his prey into helplessness. On any other man but Ki-Gor, this strategy might very well have worked, but Ki-Gor was not any other man! He did not scream, did not run, and did not cower. Ki-Gor stood his ground as the native howled and screeched before his eyes.

The native swung his machete. Ki-Gor ducked, the blade swooshing harmlessly over his head, slicing only the air! With speed honed by years of struggling to survive in the harsh jungle, Ki-Gor drew his knife and moved it upward from his crouching position, driving it into the flesh between the shrieking native's ribs! He pulled the knife out as quickly as he had plunged it in, and the attacker fell to the ground, slain instantly! Ki-Gor stood. He knew this one man had not been alone. His kind usually travelled in packs. He was right. A loud cacophony of screams cut through the air like shrapnel. Five of them appeared, charging from their cover and surrounding Ki-Gor! He was outnumbered!

Quickly, he glanced all around him, sizing up his opponents trying to come up with a strategy that might enable him to survive this confrontation. They were all naked or semi-naked. They were painted in vivid colors and grotesque designs. Some wore jewelry made of bones which Ki-Gor recognized as human bones! These were indeed the dreaded cannibals of the Forest of Dusk! As Ki-Gor glanced around, he also took note of their weapons. Two held machetes like that of the first one, whom he had already killed. Two of them held smaller daggers, and the last one wielded a long wooden staff with a round, blunt end on it. They moved closer on all sides of him now. They did not spring on him all at once, as they seemed cautious. They must have seen me slay their friend, Ki-Gor thought to himself, and they know I won't be easy prey.

Ki-Gor braced himself for the battle and the pain. He knew it wouldn't be an easy task to face five opponents at once, but he wasn't about to let them take him down easily. He silently vowed to himself that his would not be the only blood to stain the ground that day. The cannibals may have been wild and armed, but they were far from good strategists. Instead of the machete-wielding natives, with their long sharp blades attacking first, the two with the small daggers moved towards Ki-Gor. Both came at him at once, one on the left and one on the right. Luckily for Ki-Gor, both were close enough, on either side, to be within his field of vision simultaneously. He moved with lightning speed. He grabbed the wrist of the one on his left, grasping it with such strength that his opponent was unable to move the dagger towards him, or even open his hand to drop it. Ki-Gor whirled, pulling the arm of the native with him, turning towards the other dagger wielder. In one swift blur of movement, Ki-Gor drove the dagger of one cannibal into the breast of the other! The one who had been stabbed clutched his wounded chest and fell forward to the ground. The one whose motions had been directed by Ki-Gor gaped in shock at what he had just done to his companion. His stunned pause was short, only momentary, but it was long enough for Ki-Gor to take advantage of his stillness and drive his own dagger into the ribcage of the stunned one! Two down, Ki-Gor thought quickly to himself, but I'm still outnumbered.

Now the first of the machete men came charging at him. It was a clumsy assault, as he waved his weapon wildly. Ki-Gor immediately knew that this was not a very skilled fighter. Ki-Gor fell to the ground, his hands landing perfectly behind him to brace himself to the ground as he swung his legs forward to upset the footing of the charging cannibal warrior. Ki-Gor's unskilled foe fell to the jungle floor. Ki-Gor kicked the machete away, causing it to slide several feet out of range of the fallen native's reach. Then Ki-Gor pounced! When he was in semi-civilized surroundings, the man once known as Robert Kilgour could be a true gentleman, but he was nowhere near civilization now. He was deep in the wildest, most treacherous part of Africa, and here was where he could let the terrible beast within come roaring to the surface. Like a panther enraged, Ki-Gor leapt. He landed atop the cannibal and grasped the man's head in his two powerful hands. With a terrible cracking sound, he snapped his foe's neck like a brittle twig! The odds were getting better.

Before the third native's death rattle was done, Ki-Gor was back on his feet, ready to stand his ground against the next wave. Now the other machete man came at him. This one moved more slowly, more deliberately.

Ki-Gor knew this one had had more practice and would not be as easy to slay. The machete swung forward. Ki-Gor dodged. He felt the breeze as the blade just missed his scalp. He tried to jolt his own dagger forward to strike, but the cannibal was nearly as fast as he was. Each of the two fighters had now taken a stroke at the other, but no blood had yet been spilled. The machete flew forward again. Ki-Gor evaded it a second time. He was beginning to get worried. His dagger was too short, and since he and the native were of about equal height, the machete gave the cannibal the longer reach. When the next swing of the blade came, Ki-Gor dodged again and then rolled to his right. His arm shot outwards to his side and he grabbed up the machete that had belonged to the one he had already sent to hell. He jumped up and again faced his foe. Now they were evenly armed!

Clank! Clank! Clank! The machetes met in midair, striking each other, metal meeting metal. The two fought furiously with each man's attempt at slashing met and blocked by the blade of the other. Both were skilled warriors, both were at the peak of their physical conditions, and both were of roughly equal size and strength. They probably could have fought to a standstill before either of them landed a blow, but unfortunately for Ki-Gor, there was still another player in this deadly game. So focused was he on the foe in front of him, that he was unable to detect the stealthy movement behind him until it was too late. He felt the awful thud of the blunt, rounded end of that wooden staff crash down on the back of his head... and then his world went black!

The first thing Ki-Gor was aware of was the intense heat. Then came the noise; the weird, loud chanting that seemed to come from all directions. Next, he began to notice the sensations in his body. His head ached where the blow had been struck. Besides the fact that he felt intensely hot, he could feel numerous scratches and bruises all over his skin. Most odd was the way he felt like his entire body was not supporting his weight, as if he were not fully connected to the ground, but suspended somehow in the air. He realized he was still disoriented. He focused his senses. His head throbbed but he forced himself to open his eyes. As his vision cleared, the whole gruesome scene came into focus and he knew he was in a world of trouble.

He now understood why his weight and the effect of gravity had felt so distorted. He was suspended above a slowly growing fire! He was on a spit, and about to be roasted! The mock darkness of the Forest of Dusk was now added to by the true darkness of night in the jungle. The only source of light was the fire below Ki-Gor's hanging body. He could see parts of the area around him as he turned his head from side to side on his grotesque perch. The entire tribe of cannibal natives stood around the fire with ravenous greed in their eyes. Men, women and children alike eagerly awaited their evening meal...and Ki-Gor was it!

He pulled all of his senses to full alert, followed by his sharp mind. He looked at as much of the scene as he could see while simultaneously testing the tightness and strength of the thick ropes that bound him to the suspended pole. The bonds were tight and strong, and Ki-Gor could not find a weakness. He would have to think his way out of this mess.

He saw nothing but a crowd of hungry savages. He shifted his attention to the sounds around him. He could hear the crackling of the fire below him as it slowly grew hotter and hotter, beginning to singe Ki-Gor's back. He also heard the laughter and greedy snarls of the natives. Then he heard one of them speak to another, and he found hope again.

Ki-Gor knew this language! He didn't know it well, but he knew enough to understand, and perhaps to speak something resembling it, something these cannibals might understand. He suspected that it might have been a corrupted version of one of the dialects spoken by a few of the tribes he had encountered in the past. He decided to try to communicate with his captors, and maybe talk his way out of their dinner plans. He focused on the words that came into his mind, and began to try to speak their language.

"Stop, wait, listen to me!" Ki-Gor shouted.

A hush fell over the crowd of savages as they were shocked to hear recognizable words come from the mouth of a white man. One of the older villagers stepped forward.

"You speak our tongue!" said the wrinkled old cannibal.

"I do," Ki-Gor replied. "And I want you to listen to me, but let me down from here! I will no longer speak if you finish cooking me!"

The old cannibal signaled to the crowd and two large, muscled, younger natives stepped forward. They took Ki-Gor down from the pyre and held him firmly and tightly. He was still bound, but felt great relief at now being even a short distance from the heat of the flames. The two young warriors were there to make certain that he did not try to flee.

The elder cannibal, who was at least six inches shorter than Ki-Gor, looked up into the white man's eyes. "Speak now, stranger, or you go back to the fire!"

Ki-Gor laughed right in the old man's face. He knew he needed to maintain the appearance of confidence in order to convince the natives of the lies he was about to tell in order to preserve his own life.

"Why would you want to eat me?" Ki-Gor asked. "You must be foolish, desperate cannibals to resort to consuming a tough-skinned bitter old chunk of meat like me!

The elder native laughed right back at him. "You are here…and we are hungry. That is all there is to it; back to the flames with you!"

But before the two young warriors could put Ki-Gor back to the fire, he shouted out, "Wait! I can provide you with a much better meal! I can give you enough to fill the bellies of all of you…and then some! When your warriors found me alone in the jungle, I was simply scouting out the land ahead for my companions. There were a whole slew of people with me; men and women and even children! When I did not return to them, they must have assumed that I was lost and elected to take the other of the two routes we were considering. Those people mean nothing to me. I was only working for them because they were paying me. My life, of course, means more to me than money! I will gladly lead you to them if you will spare me from your fire!"

The old cannibal glared at him. "How do I know you speak the truth, white one?"

"All I can give you is my most binding oath. I swear on my own blood and honor that I speak true!" said Ki-Gor. Under any other circumstances, he would never swear a false oath, but these were savage cannibals, so they didn't count.

"These people who hired me are not warriors like me. They are soft, weak people. It would only take a few of your warriors to slay them all! I will even help, if it means sparing my own life!" added Ki-Gor.

The elder gestured to the two young natives that held Ki-Gor, and then pointed into the crowd of other villagers. It seemed he had fallen for Ki-Gor's ploy. Moments later, Ki-Gor was untied. He rubbed his sore wrists and felt the feeling return to his fingers.

"You will lead four of our young men to this group of travelers. You will help them slay them, and you will help them bring the bodies back here to be eaten. Then, if you wish, you may feast with us!" said the elder cannibal.

"One thing before we go," said Ki-Gor. "The small pouch that hung from my belt when you brought me here; where is it?" He had remembered the medicine for the priestess of Tapara.

"That, white man, will be given back to you when you return with our food!" snapped the village elder. "Now go, the five of you! The children of the village are growing hungry."

Ki-Gor and the four young cannibal warriors marched off into the jungle. Morning was approaching now and it had grown just a bit lighter, but in the Forest of Dusk, the light of dawn did not amount to much difference. The four warriors were all armed with machetes. Ki-Gor was without weapons. The cannibal villagers might have fallen for his lies, but they had not been foolish enough to give his knife back to him.

The group of five men, Ki-Gor and his four grim guardians, walked quickly, but quietly through the dense foliage of the jungle. Ki-Gor had memorized the layout of the area through which he had already traveled and used his awareness of his surroundings to lead the four cannibal warriors deep into the tree-filled lands, snaking away from the village where he had nearly met his end at their fire. They walked, and Ki-Gor waited for a good opportunity to try to break free of their company, hoping that such a chance would come before they realized that he had attempted to trick them.

The moment he had been waiting for came suddenly, about an hour into their journey. As they walked along, one of the cannibals suddenly tripped over a root that had formed a loop just inches above the ground. The unfortunate savage fell forward onto his face, knocking the wind out of him and startling his three companions. Ki-Gor did not hesitate. He pounced. His leg swept out in a strong, deliberate motion, tripping one of the other cannibals. Two were down, at least momentarily. Ki-Gor spun around and grabbed hold of the string of feathers that hung around the neck of one of the two still-standing cannibals. He used this sudden grab to whirl the native warrior right into the other standing man. The two savages, caught off-guard, were slammed into each other. They fell in a tangled heap upon the jungle floor.

The one who Ki-Gor had tripped was now trying to get up. Ki-Gor did not give him a chance, sending his foot forward with a swift and merciless kick, connecting with the cannibal's jaw, sending him reeling backwards. Now the one who had tripped to set off the whole chain of events was getting up. He had recovered from his stunning fall and had only a bloody lip to show for it. Ki-Gor tackled him. He grabbed hold of the native's machete, tearing it from his belt, and slashed it across his abdomen, killing him.

The bloody blade in hand, Ki-Gor turned to face the other three. The first of the three to reach Ki-Gor's position waved his machete wildly in the jungle lord's direction. Ki-Gor's own recently acquired weapon met the native's blade in mid-air and the two cleavers clashed together. The cannibal was strong, but Ki-Gor was stronger. The native's arm swung back

Ki-Gor and the four …warriors marched off into the jungle.

from the impact of the meeting blades and Ki-Gor took advantage of the young warrior's disadvantage to land a killing hack! Now two cannibals remained.

Ki-Gor watched them and realized that they were going to attack him in tandem. He had his doubts that he could evade two slashing machetes at once, so he opted for an alternate plan. He turned and ran, but it was no coward's flight; he had a method to his movements. He fled, and the two cannibals pursued him.

Ki-Gor ran through the jungle, leaping over rocks and fallen tree limbs. His keen mind had memorized the lay of the land over which he had already tread, so he had a picture in his head of the way he was leading the savages in pursuit of him. For half a mile he ran, and they followed, close behind, all the while stabbing and slicing at the air in vain attempts to recapture or kill him.

Finally, Ki-Gor knew that he was nearing the spot for which he aimed. A few more feet and he would be there! He jumped, anticipating what was coming up in his path. Over the suddenly appearing stream he flew! His pursuers had no idea what was under their speeding feet, and into the water they fell!

Ki-Gor heard the splash and the sudden cries of surprise, so he stopped and turned around to witness the results of his gamble. He saw the frantic splash and heard the sudden cry of pain and death as a crocodile emerged from the water and its snapping jaws stole the life of one of Ki-Gor's two foes!

The final cannibal scrambled out of the water, but had lost his weapon in the wet mud. Ki-Gor slew him quickly and easily. He took a few moments to collect his thoughts and catch his breath now that the immediate danger had been dealt with. Then he reversed his path through the Forest of Dusk, heading back towards the cannibals' village, carrying only the machete he had taken from one of those he had just killed. He had to get back to that village fast and try to get back the pouch with the healing potion made by A'Laka before those cannibals did anything to it. Then he had to be on his way again. He hoped his brief entrapment by these natives had not cost him too much time to make up.

The rest of Ki-Gor's walk back to the general vicinity of the cannibal village was uneventful. He walked at a brisk pace, but did not run. Apparently, the cannibals were all waiting back at the village for the big meal that they had been promised, but were not going to receive, as Ki-Gor saw or heard no signs of anyone moving about in the jungle as he walked. When he knew he was about half a mile from the village, he stopped walking. His sharp ears perked up and he listened for about five minutes, just making certain that nothing or no one was moving in his direction. When he was satisfied that the occupants of the village had no idea that he was so near, he began to move in their direction.

He moved slowly, methodically going a few feet at a time, keeping himself as silent as humanly possible, darting between trees and concealing himself every few paces. He took no chances, but used every possible bit of cover to his advantage. When he had arrived within a few hundred feet of the village, he climbed up into a tree and he waited. He would not try to sneak into the village until darkness arrived. As the afternoon wore on, he saw a band of about a dozen young warriors march off into the jungle. Good, he thought, they're going looking for the others. That would mean fewer natives to fight off if he happened to be spotted.

When dusk had come and gone and shadows crept upon the cannibal village, Ki-Gor could see the fires being lit in the center of the area. Apparently, it was the tribe's tradition to gather around these fires when it grew dark. He knew that now was the time to do what he had come to do.

He quietly climbed down from his tree-top perch, lay down on the ground, stolen machete in hand, and crawled on his belly towards the village. He moved slowly and made certain not to make any unnecessary sounds. Being detected would bring the whole tribe's violence down on his head, he knew, and that could well be the end of him. There would be no more opportunities to trick them.

He finally got close to the village. During his previous time there, he had noticed which hut belonged to the village chief, and he assumed that this hut would be the one where he would find what he sought.

He reached the back of the hut and stood up, bracing his body against the outer wall and being careful to not cast much of a shadow. He found an opening in the wall, a glassless window which he assumed was for ventilation. He climbed through the hole and found himself alone inside. He quickly located the small pouch that the priestess of Jorowan had given him. He attached it to his belt, where it should have been all along. He was happy to see that his own dagger was there as well. He did not see his bow or his arrows, and assumed that they had been taken for the use of the village's warriors. He would have to make do without them. He discarded the machete he had taken from the cannibal warrior and put his own knife back in his belt where it belonged. He looked around some more, rifling through piles of junk that had once been the possessions of those unfortunate enough to cross the cannibals' paths in the past. He smiled when he found one particular item; a book of matches! He looked down at the straw covered floor of the hut, and his grin grew bigger. He struck a match and dropped it, still burning, onto the floor. The fire caught easily, and the hut began to blaze! Ki-Gor snuck back out the window and ran off into the jungle, the sudden fire making a perfect distraction to keep the villagers from seeing him flee.

Ki-Gor ran through the jungle as quickly as he could, although his speed was greatly limited by the darkness of night. When he could no longer see the glow of the fire that he had started in the native village, he stopped, settled himself down against a tree, and tried to get a few hours of sleep. A lifetime of jungle living had taught Ki-Gor to sleep lightly lest some beast of prey should slay him as he slept. Still, this light sleep would be enough to refresh a man as strong and vital as the jungle lord.

The heat of the rising sun upon his cheek woke Ki-Gor as morning arrived. He did not hesitate, but sprang to his feet and was off again, traveling over the dense vegetation of the jungle floor, hoping to make up for the time he had lost in the cannibals' captivity. He travelled on for hours until his leg muscles started to cramp up and he had to slow his pace. He walked on, striding quickly, but no longer running at full speed. He had now passed the stretch of land that was known as The Forest of Dusk and the land looked much like most of the jungle did. Ki-Gor could hear the familiar songs of the jungle birds and the steady running of distant streams and rivers. He felt at home there among the thick trees and brush. The morning led into the afternoon. He estimated that he was now halfway to his destination, the village of Tapara, the twin of Jorowan.

After he had gone a little further, he paused and listened. For a moment, he thought he had heard the sound of singing. He tilted his head in the direction from which the slight jungle breeze was blowing and he concentrated on his sense of hearing. Yes, he thought, a woman's voice, raised in song!

He strained his ears to try to hear the words of the song. It sounded like the jungle dialect spoken in Jorowan! That would, Ki-Gor assumed, also be the language spoken in Tapara, though he could not be sure, since he had never visited Jorowan's sister city. Perhaps he was closer to Tapara than he had estimated, he thought. Perhaps some of the village women were out in the jungle gathering food or firewood, he suspected.

He walked in the direction of the sound. It grew louder as he progressed. It had an eerie, almost ghostly quality to it, something not quite human. It was now late afternoon and shadows were beginning to gather in the jungle, adding to the surreal atmosphere that had been created by the emergence of the singing.

He went a bit further, about half a mile, and then he came to the place where the song originated. He saw a woman, her back to him, standing in the middle of a small clearing in the jungle. She wore only a small skirt made of dried grasses. Ki-Gor saw that she had the dark skin of a jungle native, but with the slightly lighter tone of that of the people of Jorowan, and probably Tapara as well.

Ki-Gor approached her and the singing ceased. She began to turn towards him, and he gasped as he saw her face.

"A'Laka!" he exclaimed, recognizing the face of the priestess of Jorowan!

She smiled at him and he thought he saw something different about her, a subtle variation in the way her face moved, or a difference in the expression in her eyes. Then he remembered. The priestess of Tapara was A'Laka's twin! This must be the other priestess, the one he had come to save. But, he wondered, why was she out here in the jungle, singing, when she was supposedly on her deathbed?

"I had been told you were dying!" said Ki-Gor. "Your twin has sent me this way...with this!" He held up the small medicine pouch as he spoke.

The woman held out her hand in Ki-Gor's direction.

"Take my hand, and you will see that my sister spoke the truth," she said.

Ki-Gor reached for her hand, and his own hand passed right through it!

"You are a ghost! Then I am too late!" he said, and he was greatly disappointed that he had failed at his task.

"No!" she countered. "I have not left the world of mortals yet! I walk here, in this ethereal form...but the thinnest strand of connection still binds me to my body! Time has not yet run out on your quest of mercy and salvation, white man!"

Ki-Gor had never encountered a strange event like this one, but he was not entirely surprised. He had seen too many weird things in his years in the jungle to discount anything, no matter how shocking it might seem.

"The healing potion on your belt will save the life of my body...but you must first face that which has damaged my soul," the apparition continued. "Follow me now, Ki-Gor, and see that of which I speak."

"You know my name!" said Ki-Gor.

"Yes," she answered. "My connection with my sister is a strong one and

I often have knowledge of her dreams and desires, though the distance between us is a long one. She has often had fond thoughts of you, and so I know you in a way."

Then she turned and began to walk into the jungle. Ki-Gor followed her.

"My sister did not tell you my name. I am D'Nala," she said as they walked.

Ki-Gor followed the ghostly form of D'Nala for about an hour. Night had fallen and the jungle was dark again, but her eerie glow lent enough light for Ki-Gor to walk without fear of falling over the rocks and roots that dotted the ground in the random patterns of nature. They went through tree-lined trails and over patches of grass and stone. Finally, they stopped and D'Nala pointed into the jungle ahead of them.

"Do you see that small point of light through the trees?" she asked of Ki-Gor.

He saw what she was gesturing at. Through the darkness he could just make out a tiny point of yellow light, like a single candle in an otherwise night-blackened forest.

"I can go no further. My body grows weaker with each moment that I stay in this ghost-form. Follow that light and you will find the source of my sickness. Destroy what you find there…and then you may come to Tapara and complete the task of healing. You have my gratitude, Ki-Gor." With those words, the shimmering form of D'Nala, priestess of Tapara and twin sister of A'Laka of Jorowan, faded away and Ki-Gor was again alone in the depths of the jungle.

He walked on, going in the direction of the light in the distance. He could hear no unusual sounds; just the small chirping and chattering of those jungle animals that kept nocturnal hours. He could tell that he was getting closer as the small point of light began to grow more distinctly visible, so that he no longer had to strain the limits of his vision to follow it.

When he was much closer, he could see that there was a small hut, sitting alone there in the jungle, not part of any village or settlement. Who would dwell alone, here in the midst of the deepest jungle, Ki-Gor wondered? He drew a bit nearer to the hut and saw that the front was open and the light he had been following was coming from inside.

As he came within a hundred feet of the little hut, a sense of dread and malignance shook him. It was a feeling he knew well, for his jungle-honed instincts were warning him of the presence of jungle magic of the evil kind!

He knew he would have to proceed with care, trying to remain undetected until he could determine the nature of what he was about to face. He crept slowly, silently closer to the hut, using the darkness as camouflage.

He strategically moved around to the back side of the hut, hoping to find a small opening on that side, through which he could peer in and evaluate the situation before putting himself at risk. When he arrived there, he found what he sought; a small window, much like the one he had used to gain entrance to the hut of the chief cannibal.

He reached down and scooped up some dirt from the ground, smearing it on his face so that the light from within would not reflect off of his golden skin and reveal him to the hut's occupants. Then he looked in through the little window.

Inside, there was one man. He was a native of these parts, Ki-Gor judged by his appearance. He was bald-headed, tall and wiry. He had eyes that gave the impression of intelligence, but also of maliciousness, and perhaps a hint of insanity. He was dressed in a long red robe, an odd costume to see on a jungle native, so Ki-Gor assumed he had gotten it from a European visitor, either traded for or stolen. He was doing what looked like dancing, while holding a long wooden staff with an ivory head that had been carved into the shape of a snake striking at a victim. He was obviously engaged in the working of a spell or some such magic.

After Ki-Gor had evaluated the man's looks and actions, he looked around at the contents of the hut. He could see the various tools and tokens of sorcery, similar to some of the items he had seen in A'Laka's hut back in Jorowan. The hut's occupant was obviously a sorcerer of some kind, and probably not the merciful type, if D'Nala's hints had been true.

As Ki-Gor's eyes searched the hut for more information, he saw something that made it even clearer what was happening here. He looked down at the floor, beneath the dancing feet of the insane shaman, and he saw that the dancing was being done atop a painted effigy of D'Nala herself! He knew that this meant that the purpose of this dark ceremony was to do harm to the priestess of Tapara. Knowing that she was already in a weakened state, perilously close to death, Ki-Gor suspected that this might be the final stage in a series of such evil rites, meant to utterly destroy D'Nala. Knowing that any further delay might allow the culmination of the spell that was being woven, Ki-Gor resolved to act quickly and decisively.

Ki-Gor drew his dagger from his belt and ran around to the front of the hut. He stood in the front opening of the hut, bathed in the glow of the single candle that illuminated the interior, placed his hands on his hips in an effort to look as intimidating as possible, lowered his voice to a menacing snarl, and shouted, "Stop!"

The sorcerer whirled around, ceasing his mad dance and glared at Ki-Gor with anger in his eyes.

"So now the woman sends a demon to my door as a final defense!"

"I am no demon, sorcerer!" snapped Ki-Gor, "but I will defend the woman still!"

He lunged at the madman, his dagger flashing in the candlelight, but the sorcerer was faster than Ki-Gor had expected, and he lashed out with his snake-headed staff, striking Ki-Gor in the shoulder, knocking him aside and sending him crashing into a pile of ceremonial trinkets and costume pieces. The magical apparatus crunched under the weight of Ki-Gor's falling body and he could feel the crunching of bone decorations and the softness of scattering feathers under him.

He picked himself up quickly from the ground, unharmed, but surprised at the speed and strength with which the sorcerer had retaliated. Luckily, he thought, his dagger had not been knocked loose of his grip.

The two men, adrenaline rising in both their veins, stood facing each other, each ready to strike at the other. Ki-Gor moved first, lunging again at the evil shaman, but this time anticipating the swinging of the staff, and easily evading it. The staff whirled harmlessly over his head as he ducked. He tried to maneuver his dagger upward to bury it in the shaman's ribs, but the thin sorcerer took a step back and unexpectedly brought the head of his staff crashing down upon Ki-Gor's head.

Ki-Gor's last waking thought was how stupid he was for allowing himself to be struck this way again; the same way the cannibal warrior had managed to incapacitate him! He chastised himself for his mistake…and he fell into the blackness of unconsciousness.

Ki-Gor was surprised to awake. Had he been the sorcerer, he surely would have killed his victim, rather than risk keeping him alive. This sorcerer however, Ki-Gor assumed, must have had some reason for not slaying him as he lay unconscious. Now Ki-Gor sat leaning against the wall of the hut. He opened his eyes and looked up to see the sorcerer staring down at him. He tried to stand and attack, but found that he could not move.

Suddenly, Ki-Gor felt an emotion with which he was not as familiar as most men; intense, terrible fear! Ki-Gor was a man of action and movement. As long as he had his strength and his vigor, he was confident that he could find a way to survive any situation, no matter how great the odds against him, but now he found himself helpless, with a madman staring down at him!

"My mixture of herbs has done its job well, demon-man!" the insane magician gloated. "These particular plants, when combined in the right amounts, can leave one unable to move, unable to stand. You are as helpless as a baby. You will attack me no more!"

Ki-Gor was at least able to move his eyes from side to side, and in doing so he could see the light of day coming in through the opening in the hut, so he knew he had been unconscious for at least several hours.

"You interrupted my ceremony last night, demon-man," said the sorcerer, "but tonight you shall watch helplessly as I finish the task of destroying that wretched priestess. Then I will end your life, after you have seen the final destruction of the woman you serve. Once you and she are gone from this world, there will be no one to defend that little village from my magic…and I will have a little kingdom of slaves to do my bidding…and from there I will expand my domain, conquering more and more. The lengths of my power are limited only by the borders of my will!"

Good, thought Ki-Gor, at least D'Nala still lives. He wondered how long the effects of the paralyzing herbs would last. Perhaps, he thought, he might still have a small chance to succeed in his mission.

The wicked shaman turned and walked out of the hut after his bragging was finished. Ki-Gor was left sitting there by the wall of the hut. He had no idea where the shaman had gone, and he still could not move.

Hours ticked by. Ki-Gor could judge the flow of time by the way the light and the shadows crept across the floor of the hut. He could tell that morning had passed and afternoon was beginning to march by. He sat and thought about how he wanted nothing as much as he wanted to stand and strike out at the madman who had captured him, to strangle the life out of this creature of dark magic, and finish what he had come here to do.

As the day moved closer to evening, Ki-Gor felt a sudden flicker of sensation in his shoulders. The drug must be wearing off, he thought! He could feel the aching of his muscles begin to travel down his arms. Slowly, the feeling was returning to his body. It seemed like an eternity before he was able to move his fingers just slightly. Then the sensations began to return to his legs as well. Finally, he got up and stood! He found the medicine pouch and the dagger against the opposite wall of the hut. He walked about a bit, stretched his aching limbs to cure himself of the last remaining stiffness that had been the result of being immobile for so long. Finally, as

...he found himself helpless with a madman staring down at him.

dusk settled over the jungle, his ears picked up the sound of footsteps not far away, and he knew that the sorcerer was returning.

Ki-Gor went back to the place where he had sat against the wall for so long. He hid the dagger and pouch behind him, hoping that the sorcerer would not notice that they had been taken back from the place where he had left them. Then Ki-Gor let his body go limp, imitating the posture in which he had been held for so long. It was obvious to him that his captor had overestimated the length of time for which he would be paralyzed, or he would not have left him there alone for so long.

Ki-Gor waited there, and ten minutes later, the madman returned. He had gathered more herbs and roots while he had been away, and he tossed them in a heap in the corner of the hut. He looked down at Ki-Gor and smiled wickedly at him, wordlessly gloating.

Ki-Gor watched, still feigning paralysis, as the shaman sat down and ate some of the plants he had gathered. As he feasted, night fell and the small hut grew darker, until the shaman finally lit his candle again.

After eating, the shaman stood up, took out the parchment with the painted image of D'Nala, and placed it in the center of the hut's floor. He knelt over it and his eyes began to grow strangely wild, as if he were in the process of putting himself into some sort of trance. His lips began to move and Ki-Gor, from his seated position, listened to the strange, guttural sounds that came from the sorcerer's lips. They were not even words, but sounded more like the savage, primal pleadings of a primitive animal-man to some dark and formless deity. Ki-Gor was glad that he did not know how to translate those terrible sounds into any language that he knew.

After nearly an hour of the weird chanting and the swaying that accompanied it, the shaman stood. He looked down at the picture of the priestess, and he spat on it! Ki-Gor's rage grew as he watched the sorcerer's actions, but he did not move. The time was not yet right.

The shaman looked up at the ceiling of the hut, and he began to make those sounds again, louder this time, more frantic. He gazed at the ceiling, but it looked as if he were looking through the straw roof and into the blackness of the sky, and even beyond, into the depths of space, begging for the assistance of some terrible force beyond human comprehension. The evil tone of his noises was beginning to make Ki-Gor's blood boil.

The sorcerer's trance appeared to be growing deeper and deeper and Ki-Gor knew that now was the time to make his move. He slowly, so as not to attract attention immediately, let his hands slide behind him, to use them to propel his body forward when the second of attack arrived. He wrapped the fingers of one hand around the handle of his dagger. He took in a deep breath and focused all his muscles to the task before him…and he pounced!

Like the mighty lion who he had watched slay the lumbering warthog days earlier, Ki-Gor flew across the hut, his teeth clenched, his voice growling, his dagger flashing! He tackled the shaman to the floor, knocking him out of his gruesome, self-induced trance, slamming him against the rear wall of the small dwelling. The wall gave way to the force of two bodies colliding with it, and Ki-Gor and his foe crashed to the ground outside.

The sorcerer howled in rage. This time he had no staff with which to defend himself. His fingernails clawed at Ki-Gor, missing the eyes, but ripping gashes down the sides of his face. The shaman's face was twisted with terrible anger, like that of a man possessed by the foulest of demonic forces. He spat out words in some ancient, long-forgotten language that Ki-Gor had never heard before, but there was no mistaking the meaning. Those utterances could be nothing but the vilest of curses.

Ki-Gor swung his dagger around, going for the shaman's throat, but the wiry, but strong hand of the sorcerer caught him by the wrist. The shaman tried to turn Ki-Gor's dagger back towards the heart of its owner, but Ki-Gor pulled his arm to the side, not tearing free of the shaman's grip, but shaking the dagger from his own hand, letting it fly off to the side of the place where they wrestled. It was better to fight on unarmed, Ki-Gor had decided; than to let an opponent use my own knife to kill me!

The two men tumbled over several times, grappling for control in the dirt and grass of the jungle floor, each gaining and then losing the advantage several times. Finally, Ki-Gor had had enough. He decided to use every ounce of his strength and end this conflict now. He let out a furious growl; sounding more like a jungle beast than any other man could possibly sound. The sudden, terrible outburst from Ki-Gor's mouth shocked the shaman for just a second, just enough to make his straining muscles lapse in their efforts.

Ki-Gor took full advantage of the opportunity he had just provided for himself. He used his hands to pin the shaman's hands to the ground at his sides. The shaman tried to push Ki-Gor off of him, but his efforts only resulted in Ki-Gor slamming his own head forward, butting the shaman in the face! Blood exploded from the sorcerer's broken nose, and Ki-Gor felt a burst of grim satisfaction at finally having made the madman bleed!

Ki-Gor grabbed hold of the bleeding shaman, grasping him even harder by the shoulders and pulled him along with him as he rolled over again, rolling in the direction of the place where his dagger had landed moments earlier. The shaman let out one last desperate gasp of terror as he saw what Ki-Gor was reaching for. It was the last sound that would ever intentionally come from the demented magician's mouth, followed only by the gurgling rattle of death as the sharp blade of Ki-Gor's knife sank up to its hilt in the shaman's side.

The body of the sorcerer went limp, and he was dead. Ki-Gor retrieved his weapon from its place between the dead man's ribs, thinking for a moment of a story his wife, Helene, had told him of a young English boy who had pulled a sword from a stone to claim a crown.

He sunk the blade into the ground for a moment, cleansing the foul blood of the sorcerer from its metallic surface before putting it back in his belt where it belonged. Then the jungle lord stood up, walked back through the hole their fighting bodies had torn in the hut's wall, and retrieved the little pouch of magical medicine for what felt like the thousandth time. He put it next to the knife in his belt. Then he took the shaman's still lit candle and set fire to the hut of horrors. He turned his back to the blazing hut and walked back into the jungle from which he had come.

Ki-Gor walked until the flames of the burning hut were only a pale glow in the background. Then he found a tall, straight tree and sat leaning against it, and he slept.

Morning came and Ki-Gor stood once again. He climbed to the top of the tallest tree he could find and looked out to the horizon, judging the terrain below in order to figure out exactly where he was. Good, he told himself, I'm not far now. He estimated that he was only one more day's walk from Tapara. He walked quickly, but did not run, as his body ached from the ordeal of the past few days. He went on for several hours, and then stopped to eat some berries and drink from the cold, fresh stream that ran through this part of the jungle. After the short break, he resumed his journey.

Afternoon inched by and he made good time. As he travelled on, the thickness of the jungle began to subside and he knew he was nearing his destination. Finally, he could hear the voices that travelled through the air when one came within a small distance of a fairly large settlement. Tapara, he whispered to himself, and he quickened his pace a bit.

He reached the borders of the little town and the people looked up from their daily tasks, their eyes growing wide with wonder at the sight of this tall, muscular white man with pale blonde hair emerging from the surrounding jungle.

One of the village's young warriors walked over to great him.

"The village priestess has been awaiting your arrival," said the youth, in the shared language of Tapara and Jorowan. "Come with me."

Moments later, Ki-Gor found himself entering a hut that was eerily similar to the one he had been in when he had agreed to undertake this mission of salvation. He walked inside and was met by a large bald man who could have been Luther's brother. It turned out to be not his brother, but his cousin, as the aides of the priestesses were determined by blood-lines just as the priestesses were.

The man did not say anything, but gestured to the bed of furs at the back of the hut. On this bed lay the body of D'Nala, still and weak looking, but gently breathing. Ki-Gor had arrived while she still lived, and the sight brought a small smile to his face.

He walked over to her.

"Priestess?" he said gently. "D'Nala?"

A soft sound came as her lips parted slightly. It was like the murmuring of one who is lost in a deep dream.

Now her aide spoke. "You have the potion of healing?" he asked.

Ki-Gor was about to hand the little pouch to the man, but the man shook his head.

"No," he said. "It is the messenger who must give it to her. You must do it. Open the bag, place it at her lips, and give life back to her."

Ki-Gor knelt beside the bed. He opened the top of the small pouch and he held it over D'Nala's face. He stroked her cheek lightly, hoping to wake her enough for her to take what he offered.

"Priestess," he said. "You must take this. It is from your twin."

She opened her eyes slightly, and she smiled at him.

"The evil one...is he dead?" she asked softly.

"His vile blood stained my dagger," said Ki-Gor in reply.

The priestess smiled.

"Then my soul is safe. Now my body must heal as well."

She reached up and wrapped her fingers around the little pouch. Ki-Gor released it from his grip, letting her take it for herself.

She poured the contents of the pouch into her mouth. It looked like a fine powder or dust as it tumbled from the pouch into her mouth. She coughed once and looked over at her assistant.

"Water," she gasped.

The tall, bald man took a water skin from his belt and gave it to her. She drank greedily, in long full gulps, the handed it back to him. She reclined on the bed and fell back into her sleep.

"Will she be all right?" Ki-Gor wondered aloud.

"Even the most potent of magic takes time, my friend," said her assistant. "Now she must rest. Come with me."

The two men left the little hut and went back into the midst of the village.

"My name is Gruttor," said the bald man, and he shook Ki-Gor's hand. "You are hungry, I think."

Ki-Gor nodded and soon found a lavish meal of fresh gazelle meat in front of him. He ate the meat and drank some French wine that the villagers had bartered for. He felt refreshed after his long trip and he took a late afternoon nap with the sounds of the village children laughing and playing in the background.

When he woke up, it was night again and torches lit the avenues between the many small huts of Tapara. Seeing that Ki-Gor was awake, Gruttor walked over and smiled down at him.

"She is awake, and she wishes to see you," he told Ki-Gor.

They went back to the hut of the priestess. When they entered, Ki-Gor was delighted to see that D'Nala was standing on her own. She looked much better than she had earlier and Ki-Gor was glad.

"My sister made a good choice of messengers," she said as she smiled at Ki-Gor. "Her potion was a potent one, and it has done its work." She reached out and took hold of Ki-Gor's hand.

"Tell me, brave one," she continued, "do you have a mate?"

Ki-Gor laughed out loud. "You recover quickly! You are very much like your sister!"

"And you have known the pleasure of my sister's company then?" she asked him.

"I have, but it was long ago," said Ki-Gor.

"Then perhaps you are due to know of the talents of our family line once more," she said seductively.

"No," said Ki-Gor. "That was before I had one who calls me husband. My heart, priestess, belongs to someone now, and it always will."

D'Nala shook her head in disappointment.

"A pity," she said. "Should you ever change your mind, I shall be here, with gratitude in my heart...and my body. Now let us go and join my people in celebration of your deeds of bravery!"

The whole village was in revelry that night. The people drank and feasted, consuming the amount of food that would normally sustain them for a week or more. Songs were sung and tales of brave ancestors related around the blazing fires. The women of the village danced for the pleasure of the men, and then the men did the same for the women. All were happy and it was a welcome respite from the usual harsh reality of life in the jungle of Africa.

In the morning, Ki-Gor set out on the long journey home. He would have an easier time of it on the return trip. The grateful people of Tapara had given him two skins, one of water and one of wine, and a supply of food for his travels. It would be an easier trip, but a somewhat longer one, as he would take a different route this time, avoiding The Forest of Dusk and its savage cannibal tribes. He would move along the coast, perhaps visiting several villages that he had previously been to. He would doubt-lessly encounter some European traders and merchants and would perhaps trade some information or advice, based upon his vast knowledge of this land, in exchange for some small gift to present to his wife upon his return. He would also be sure to make a stop in Jorowan on his way home, to tell Luther and A'Laka of his journey and its successful completion, although he was sure that A'Laka was already aware of her twin's renewed vitality.

It had been a long and perilous journey, but the happiness on the faces of the people of Tapara had been enough to make it a worthwhile mission for Ki-Gor. He truly loved the ways of jungle life and was always happy to come to the aide of the peaceful tribes of his adopted continent. The ways of his forefathers, the Scottish, held some minor interest for him, if only for their strangeness. Though he had been born of European descent, the ways of those people were alien to him. He never thought of himself as anything other than a creature of the jungle. It was here, in Africa, that he had grown to manhood, where he lived, and where he would someday meet his end and that was good enough for him.

He began his long walk away from Tapara, looking back only once, to see the village children waving at him. He waved back, then turned his back and strode into the jungle again, not knowing if he would ever have occasion to come to this land again.

Soon any sign of human life was behind him and he was surrounded by the sights and sounds of all the other inhabitants of the jungle. He could hear the chattering of the monkeys and the cawing of the brightly-colored birds that flew high above the treetops. The roots and leaves crunched un-der his feet as he walked, and somewhere in the distance he heard the fierce growl of a mighty lion, perhaps about to lead his pride in a charge against some prey. He could hear the sound of running water off to the east and the thunderous footsteps of a herd of rhinos to the west. This was the music that made his heart swell with joy. He walked on and on, vowing to stop only when he had to eat or sleep. The sooner he was back home and with Helene again, the better.

Many miles from the travelling jungle lord, A'Laka sat up in bed. She let out a strong, satisfied sigh.

"Luther!" she called out, commanding the attendance of her loyal aide.

The tall, heavyset, bald man came bounding into her hut, a look of worry etched upon his dark face.

"What is it my priestess?" he said, fearing that her illness had grown worse.

A'Laka let out a shriek of delight as she got to her feet and whirled about in a little dance of joy before Luther's startled yes.

"It is done, Luther, it is done!" she said with joy. "My sister lives! Ki-Gor did as we asked! Let the people know of this. Today will be a day of celebration, Luther, and we shall have another such day when Ki-Gor again graces our village with his presence. What a brave one he is, Luther! I wish he didn't have a mate!"

And Luther walked out of the hut and went among the people of the village and he roared out in his great, booming voice of how Ki-Gor had once again done what most men would find impossible to do, and on that night, the people of Jorowan danced as the people of Tapara had.

THE END

Welcome to the Jungle

A frica of the 1930s; what a perfect setting for an adventure story! There are reasons why this particular place and time are so well suited for this kind of fiction. The fictional version of Africa, at that time, was right on the edge of the end of its long age of mystery, and circumstances of past and present combined to make it a great stage for drama and action and suspense. The modern era had started to touch the "dark continent" and so it had become reachable. Thanks to the increasing efficiency of air and sea travel, almost anyone could get to Africa if they so desired. This helps out a writer tremendously. Given an airplane or a ship, we can find almost any sort of character plopped down in the middle of the land of jungles, desserts, and cannibals. Whether British, French or American, male or female, civilian or military, they just might find their way to Africa. That's one advantage of the era. The second great thing about it lies in the opposite direction. While we could get there, it was still easy to get lost in the mystery of it all. The world had not shrunk yet. There was no instant communication via cell phones, no GPS navigation, no satellites and cable news networks and all the other things that make the world seem smaller than ever before. Sure, it was easy to get to Africa, but heaven help you once you got there! You might still get lost there, amid the jungle and the darkness and the danger!

In writing my Ki-Gor story, I had a lot of influences running through my mind. I'd like to mention some of them here. Ian Fleming might have been involved in this. I'm not quite certain if he was or not. If he was, the influence was unconscious on my part. After writing the beginning of this story, which starts with a lion and a warthog, it occurred to me that Fleming had started *Diamonds Are Forever* in a similar fashion, except that he had used a scorpion and a beetle. Now I wasn't thinking of that scene when I wrote mine, but since I had read Fleming's works about 15 years earlier, some portion of my mind may have pulled the scene from my memory of that. So I owe some credit, if indeed any is due, to Ian Fleming. The influence of Edgar Rice Burroughs should be obvious, as one can hardly think of jungle heroes without his work coming to mind. However, I read

Burroughs only recently in my life. I'm probably far more indebted to the Tarzan movies than the books. I used to watch the movies when they were shown on Sunday afternoon TV. I haven't seen any of them in many years, but bits and pieces of images are still burned in my memory. Robert E. Howard must also be mentioned. Some of my favorite stories to be set in the jungle are the tales of Solomon Kane. And I have to mention the great Joe Kubert, who illustrated many of the finest jungle-based stories ever to appear in comic books.

Finally, I would like to dedicate this story to my grandfather, who understands, more than anyone else I know, the appeal of the jungle adventure genre. As a child, he read every issue of *Jungle Comics* that he could find. And then there's the great story about him that I heard years ago. It seems that when he was a little boy, he went to see one of the early Tarzan movies one Saturday morning. He was so inspired by the film that he went up to the woods that bordered the streets where he lived, took off all his clothes, and went running around playing Tarzan...until some concerned citizen caught sight of him and called the cops! I wonder how my great-grandparents reacted when a policeman showed up at their door with a naked kid in tow! I hope they weren't too hard on him. He was just a kid with a freshly inspired imagination, and there are few things in the world that are better than that.

The Africa of the '30s might be gone forever, and that is probably a good thing. Progress, as much as some people fear it, usually works out all right in the long run. But the Africa that exists in fiction will never completely fade away; not as long as there are writers willing to visit it, and children willing to dream.

AARON SMITH – is a veteran writer of mysteries and pulp fiction. He has written stories featuring such characters as Sherlock Holmes, Dan Fowler: G-Man, Wild Bill Hickok, the Three Mosquitoes, and the Black Bat. He is (as far as he's been able to find out) the first author to write a novel featuring Doctor John Watson without Sherlock Holmes (*Season of Madness*). He holds a position as a staff writer for the Pro Se Productions line of pulp magazines. He has also written a science-fantasy novel, *Gods*

and Galaxies. Characters created by Smith include Hound-Dog Harker, the Red Veil, and Detective Lieutenant Marcel Picard.

Aaron Smith counts among his biggest influences as a writer Sir Arthur Conan Doyle, Roger Zelazny, JRR Tolkein, HP Lovecraft, Stan Lee (and all his collaborators), Bram Stoker, Gene Roddenberry, Ian Fleming, and many others.

THE DEVIL'S NEST

By Duane Spurlock

There is always something new out of Africa. (*Ex Africa semper aliquid novi.*)
—Pliny the Elder paraphrasing Aristotle

The Congo Jungles

An arrow thudded into the tree bole three inches from Ki-Gor's face. That was his signal to move. *Now.*

He didn't even flinch before suddenly flowing into motion: One moment he was still, the second he was rushing up the same tree trunk the arrow had struck—lithe and fluid as a leopard, leaping upward, seeming to touch a limb only slightly before flying to the next branch, reaching out to a liana, swinging into space, landing in the crotch of another massive tree. He didn't seem to pause for a second, but flew through the arms of the trees like a continually moving breeze.

All the while, arrows flashed by Ki-Gor, directed from the jungle floor. He twisted, dove from limbs of one great height to another, feinted, whipped behind trunks, sped along massive branches. All the while, his passage was silent but for the rustle of a disturbed leaf, the scuff of his foot sole across tree bark, and the *whick-whick-whick* of arrows through the air.

The blond-haired jungle man—who seemed more creature than man in this display of his prowess—never ceased to move during this aerial ballet.

Until he hesitated—just momentarily—when the sound of laughter reached his ears.

Feminine laughter, reaching him as he danced through the sky-stretching limbs of giant trees. Laughter he recognized.

In that split-second pause, an arrow—one of all the dozens shot in his direction—smacked the calf of his left leg.

Ki-Gor whipped through the air and scrambled down trees until he reached the ground, panting, to stand before the figure who laughed so heartily at him.

Helene. The beautiful red-haired woman to whom Ki-Gor had pledged his love for life.

"What is so funny?" the man asked.

Helene stifled her laughter to say, "My dear, you can't impress me if I'm not here to see you perform."

A puzzled frown showed on Ki-Gor's face. "Impress you? How?"

"Why, this marvelous display—flying through the trees, evading GTongo's arrows," she said.

At that moment, GTongo and two others joined Helene and Ki-Gor. "We were just seeing who was the best bowman of GTongo's family— GTongo or his sons," the jungle man said. He frowned again. "Until you showed up, none of them was best." He wiped a red smear from the spot the arrow had struck his leg—for none of the arrows shot at Ki-Gor had been barbed, but were simply shafts carrying a blob of dye made from local leaves and berries.

"Red—I am the best!" shouted GTongo, because the shafts used by his sons had been daubed with blue and green dye. The father wagged a finger at NGonto and NTongo. "You'll pay more attention during your lessons, now, won't you?"

Ki-Gor continued, as if he'd not been interrupted: "No one is impressing anyone here. This is about skill and staying alive in the jungle. It's peaceful now, but there are plenty of beasts out there who want to kill us. Some with four legs, some with two."

Helene laughed again. The antics of Ki-Gor and his friends were, she knew, quite serious. But they reminded her of the games men played in the civilized world she'd known before coming to the jungle, where Ki-Gor had captured her heart, and where she'd decided to spend the rest of her life. But the games of civilized men usually were played against some sort of darker background of brinksmanship—she'd seen men win and lose fortunes and reputations in a deal of cards, roll of dice, or race of horses. Here in the jungle, Ki-Gor and his friends put great effort into their playing, but with all the innocence and seriousness of boys. Keeping skills honed here in the world of tooth and claw meant staying alive a bit longer, protecting loved ones better; but seeing these grown men running, leaping, and attacking reminded Helene of watching bear cubs tumbling together, learning how to fight and survive with a playfulness that displayed their simple but effervescent joy for living.

She felt her heart swell with love for this world, for the friends she'd made here, and for the love she carried for Ki-Gor. Helene suddenly put her arms around his neck and hugged tightly.

GTongo smiled, and his sons laughed. "Hey," Ki-Gor protested, "helping GTongo get me with an arrow wasn't enough? Are you waiting for someone to stick me with a knife now?" Then he, too, began to laugh. Having this beautiful woman here in his arms, warm and so full of life, wasn't so bad. Maybe she'd been impressed after all.

Helene chuckled, released Ki-Gor. "If you're through with your little games," she said, "then you can help me prepare for our trip."

"Trip?"

"We're going to visit Tchamba's tribe. We're leaving today."

"It takes a day to get there. We just saw them during the last moon."

"But I just learned his wife is going to have a baby." A fresh delight shone on the woman's face.

"A baby!" Ki-Gor winked at GTongo. "I hope it is a boy—there are far too many women in Tchamba's tribe. Is the baby coming soon?"

Helene rolled her eyes. "No, not for many more weeks."

The puzzled look returned to Ki-Gor's face. "Then why are we going now?"

Helene put her fists on her hips. "Because that's part of having a baby—before the baby arrives, the women sit around and chatter and laugh and talk about how wonderful the baby will be. And it's very important to reassure the mother that even if the baby is a boy, there's an excellent chance he will be far smarter than his father."

GTongo and his sons released great belly laughs now.

"All right," Ki-Gor gave in, "let's get ready and go. But I don't see how this baby will get any benefit from such monkey chattering if he's not even here to hear it."

"You have your skills, Ki-Gor, and I have mine." She turned and walked away.

Yes, Ki-Gor thought as he watched her lithe beauty flow into the surrounding trees, she's right. And he followed right along, leaving GTongo, NGonto, and NTongo to their laughter.

Paris

"The times of our world are unstable, swiftly changing; but the world's treasures are timeless." So said the man—tall and stout, dressed in a blood-red silk gown decorated with Oriental dragons and swirls that ran down to the floor and covered all but the toes of his black slippers—standing at the window. His face was lit from streetlamps outside, for the room he stood in was dark.

He turned toward the room's interior, and the light flowed like a living serpent across the folds of his gown, blazed in a sudden flash from his monocle. "Governments change, state borders shift, but treasure belongs to whoever has the stronger grasp." He smiled.

The man to whom Caspar Kovacevich spoke was tall and lean, and though he appeared relaxed at the moment while he lit a cigarette, his crisp movements and the sharp focus of his gaze gave evidence he could snap into violent action with less than a moment's notice. Martin Grainger exhaled a cloud of blue smoke, then said, "You've made these points clear before, Mr. Kovacevich. I remain at your service because I've seen the truth in your words."

Kovacevich continued smiling as he seated his bulk in a leather-upholstered chair whose ample size was enough to envelop even his great stature. He gestured to a boy, perhaps ten years old, who sat at a table contemplating a chess board—the pieces of which were positioned as in the middle of a game. The boy stood by the chair. The wave and color of his hair, the shape of his eyes demonstrated his kinship to Kovacevich.

The seated man took one of the boy's hands in his own. "My son and I rely upon the efficiencies and effectiveness of your service, Martin. Gregor and I enjoy the luxuries available to us only because you serve us so well. And it is your abilities that keep me calling on you."

"I've never taken lightly your confidence in me, Mr. Kovacevich." Where Caspar's French was fluid as a native Parisian, Grainger's carried a slight touch of British inflection.

Caspar patted Gregor on the head, then pointed to a black enameled box on a shelf across the room. The boy brought it to his father. The box was roughly a foot square in size.

Kovacevich removed the lid and took from within what looked like a large potato or lump of rock, eight inches tall. However, where the light from the street touched the object, it shone with the gleam of polished gold.

"Do you read your Bible, Martin?"

"Not in many years, Mr. Kovacevich."

"There is much to learn there. Not only about the wrath of God and His mercy, but about the treasures of this world that men grasp." He admired the gold. "The first commandment Moses received from God at Mount Sinai was, '*Tu n'auras pas d'autres dieux devant ma face.*' Thou shalt have no other gods before me. Now, Martin, I have studied the Bible, and I have determined I am a fallen creature living in a fallen world. I love the treasures of this world, and my human pride—a foolish thing, I admit, in the face of holiness and divinity—will not let me humble myself before God. I want *this* world's treasures, not those of the next world." Kovacevich paused again. "You know, of course, about King Solomon?"

Martin Grainger nodded.

"He asked God for wisdom. Yahweh also bestowed great riches on King David's son." Caspar gazed at the rock a moment. "Gold from Ophir came repeatedly to Solomon as tribute and for building and maintaining the first Temple. Ophir has been thought by some to be as legendary as Atlantis—no one has determined its location in all these centuries. No one has found it." He lifted the rock in Martin's direction, and the light revealed one grouping of the rough spots along its side to be somewhat regular, like ideograms cut into its surface. "This marred ingot came from Ophir. Because of these marks, and extensive researches and inquiries, I know where the mines may be found."

Grainger, seemingly imperturbable, raised his eyebrows.

"You'll go there, Martin. Take a select group you can trust to secure it. And I'll hold it, Martin, with a strong grasp that no government will shake loose, and they'll have to deal with me on my terms. I like my lifestyle, Martin, and I'll protect Gregor and myself no matter what armies march today or tomorrow or ten years from now. Ophir's gold shall be mine."

"Where will I be going, Mr. Kovacevich?"

"To the Congo."

Boston

"Are you unwell, Mr. Felton?"

The speaker appeared to have been cast for a play from Dickens: there was something Victorian about his speech; his clothes, though custom tailored and impeccable in their quality, were of a style slightly out of fashion; and his features verged on caricature—a large, domed head with bulging eyes perched on a thin neck, connected to a gaunt frame that might be mummifying itself as though to steal profit from some expert in mortuary sciences who eagerly awaited the day George Duke Buckingham's name appeared in the local obituaries.

On the contrary, Mr. Buckingham was quite healthy and expected to thrive beyond the celebration of his one hundredth birthday.

However, John Edward Felton, the stout and healthy young man to whom he spoke, appeared pale and nervous.

"No, Mr. Buckingham, I'm fine, sir."

"You appear feverish."

"No, sir, I'm fine, thank you."

"Very well. Mr. Rockwell Barnes, I must say, is not fine. He is ailing, and he does not expect to last the year. And so he has engaged our firm to locate his only son and heir, Brendan Barnes."

Buckingham said "our firm" as if unaware his sole partner, Mr. George Villiers Dumas, Esquire, had died two decades ago.

"Brendan Barnes, sir?" Felton questioned.

"We have been the elder Barnes' attorneys since before the younger Barnes' birth. Brendan Barnes disappeared into the Congo a decade past on some sort of ethnographical tomfoolery." Buckingham wove his fingers together. The room was dim, as if the light came from a time older even than the man's clothing, for the shutters were closed. "We are to engage an agent to find Brendan Barnes, inform him of his father's imminent demise and his subsequent assumption of the Barnes estate, and return with the young man to Boston. I want you to engage the agent for this mission."

Felton's nervousness diminished. "When did Mr. Barnes last hear from his son?"

"When he left for the jungle, after arriving in Dakar."

"He's had no word since?"

"None."

"He may be dead!"

Buckingham frowned at this burst of emotion as though it indicated insolence. "The agent's mission will include determining by gathering whatever evidence possible whether, in the event the younger Barnes may not be found, the son may be deceased. All our efforts must be expedited, for as I mentioned, the elder Barnes expects to join the Great Unknown in the coming months. On with you."

Felton nodded and left the vast room—from which he had never seen Buckingham leave; indeed, he had never seen Buckingham other than seated behind his desk—and sat at his desk in a cramped office off the hallway leading to the reception parlor and waiting room.

Felton pulled a large leather-bound notebook from a drawer and flipped it open. He needed to contact the company in London the firm used for dealing with international matters, such as this Barnes business. There was the Belgian embassy to telegraph . . .

The young man paused.

He'd looked pale and nervous to Mr. Buckingham, but he'd said he was fine.

He'd lied.

He had been pale and nervous. His interest in his new assignment had distracted him momentarily from his worries.

He had worries because last night he'd sat before a particularly ugly individual named Joe the Shark. Joe's teeth weren't sharpened to points, but the impression that they were wouldn't leave the mind of whoever had to sit before him, flecked by his spit as Joe berated him and demanded payment for egregious gambling debts.

Like Felton had endured. The thing about Joe stuck in Felton's mind was an image of the thug's teeth.

Gnashing. Sharp.

Felton's reputation was on the cusp of being ruined, his family's standing in the community undermined, because Felton was a spoiled brat who liked acting the big man, who liked to be hep with the other flash young men who visited blind pigs or even more disreputable establishments. Most damaging was Felton's inability to resist a bet. His father's influence had gotten him this clerk's position with Buckingham in the hope that experiences in the legal field under the mentorship of the gaunt attorney would help the young fool find his place, mature, and earn favor in the eyes of an esteemed legal expert who—surely some day, as a recognition of mortality finally dawned—would eventually take another partner to ascend to ownership over the firm in the event of Buckingham's death. Or at least retirement.

The clerk had been pale and more than nervous last night in the face of Joe the Shark's teeth and wrath. Felton had gripped the splintered sides of the chair in which he sat to keep from sobbing aloud.

Because Felton couldn't resist a bet—because he was callow and undisciplined—he owed Joe the Shark money. Lots of money. Money he didn't have to hand, money he knew his father wouldn't extend to him.

Now he saw an opportunity. A risk, yes, but that was the way it went with a spoiled young fool who couldn't resist a gamble. Barnes perhaps had an heir. Perhaps not. What if someone else made that determination before the authorized representative of the elder Barnes had a chance to do so? What if, for instance, a representative of Joe the Shark could make sure that Joe ended up with the money that might otherwise have gone to an heir who, after all, may already be deceased?

Certainly the person who put Joe the Shark on that trail would have erased a debt, right?

Felton took from another drawer a smaller book. He opened it, found a number. Felton still would call the London firm. But first he would place another call. A call to Joe the Shark.

Sudan

From a distance, it appeared a devil was kicking up a dust storm. A much closer view, however, revealed a troop of open touring cars rolling quickly across the dusty plains.

In the first of the three vehicles, Billy McShane, an American soldier of fortune, drove. Beside him sat Martin Grainger. Despite the automobile's speed, billows whirled and enveloped the men in its seats. Billy hacked and gagged on occasion. Martin ignored his protests.

A day earlier, Billy had asked, "Why are we killing ourselves driving these Dodge cars in the middle of nowhere? Camels or horses, mules, anything is better than this."

Martin's expression hadn't changed. "They were good enough for that dinosaur hunter in the Gobi, they're good enough for me here," he said.

"Did they choke to death, too?"

Martin remained silent. Billy could be a complainer, but he was a great one with a gun and knife. Using one of the American's words, Billy had *grit*.

Today, Martin and his band were on the lookout—as best they could through the dust—for a gang of brigands. His inquiries in the north had led him to believe the men he sought should be in the area, and Martin expected to make contact soon. Perhaps today.

A bullet slammed into Martin's door.

"Stop!" he cried.

"Hell's bells, Grainger, they're shooting at us!"

"Stop!"

Billy braked, and the two cars behind stopped as well. Their shadowing cloud rolled off to the east.

On a rise of ground just west of the cars stood a dozen men with guns trained on the vehicles.

"These are our boys," Martin said. "Keep the engine running, just in case." Billy frowned as Martin opened his door and stepped out. He waved a large white bandanna overhead.

The men on the ridge appeared to confer a few moments. As Martin began walking toward the group, three stepped away and met him halfway.

The largest, with a face like a jackal and broad shoulders over which were looped a bandolier bright with brass cartridges, spoke first: "What do you want to tell me before I kill you and take your motor vehicles?"

Martin neither smiled nor grimaced. Dust caked his face, giving him the appearance of a desert demon clothed in khaki. "If you kill me, you won't know how to operate these cars. And you will forfeit a greater gift, which will anger your master."

"Who says I have a master?"

"I seek Ali Mohammed Wau. From what I know, he is wiser than to wander these wastes looking for fools to rob. He sends his strongest men for that."

A note of slyness slipped into the big raider's tone. "Why do you seek Ali?"

"That I will explain only when I see his face and he sees mine. Lead on." Martin turned and trudged to the waiting cars.

The big thief scowled at the back so boldly turned toward him. "He dares much."

One of his companions asked, "What shall we do?"

"We will take him to Ali, who will have us kill him. And I will drive one of those machines and drag that one's corpse across the stones until not even the jackals will have enough left to lick." They returned to the ridge.

The horsemen formed a loop around the three autos and led the group to a camp of some fifty tents ten miles away from the site of their encounter. Once they stopped, men with guns closed around the vehicles, outside of which stood Martin's men with their own guns at the ready. Martin had been shown into the largest tent—that of Ali Mohammed Wau—where wary introductions already had been made.

The bandit leader's scrutiny of his visitor was sharp as a hawk's. His smile was closer to a predatory sneer than to an expression of mirth or pleasure.

"Why do you seek me, infidel?"

He shot to the heart of matters: "Why do you seek me, infidel?"

Martin bowed. "Two things, Ali. My inquiries and research across this country tell me, first, that you are a great warlord among bandits. Thieves from distant journeys kill one another to out-perform their rivals in stealing treasures, that they may be found worthy of joining your ranks."

"That is one thing."

"Second is this, which depends upon the answer to a question."

The warlord's gaze hardened. "The question?"

Martin didn't hesitate. "Are you *ashraf*?"

Ali's sneer appeared to sharpen. "We are *ashraf*."

Martin bowed again. He knew how to flatter the bandit leader diplomatically by calling him noble born and descended from Muhammad. "Then my studies tell me Ali Mohammed Wau is the Mahdi."

One of Ali's eyes twitched. "You put your weight on unstable sand, infidel. You are near to death."

The Englishman's confidence did not fail. "You are a great leader, Ali. Men of strength and daring flock to your side already. Once the word is spread—by those mysterious but lightning-quick ways information moves across the desert—that you are the Mahdi, even more daring men shall join you in great throngs to do your will. Your power will expand in this country—already there are struggles among those who want the British to stay, the British to go, and this instability will help you gather men and strength to become the destiny for your people."

Martin didn't read his Bible, but he knew his history and the rough currents of this country's opinions about who should govern it. The uprising by the last man who had declared himself Mahdi had shaken the region and fiercely tested the mettle of the British Army in the 1880s and '90s.

Caspar Kovacevich's agent knew if he could stir Ali into building a destabilizing insurrection, so much attention would be focused on this corner of the Sudan that Martin could pass southward on his mission—virtually invisible—into the Congo.

Finally Ali Mohammed Wau spoke. "You tell me this. Why are you here?"

"I see how your men are outfitted. They are brave, hard warriors, true. But their weapons—rifles left behind from the Great War, odds and ends picked up in raids. I saw 1916 Berthier carbines that probably jam on grit and sand more often than they fire. For your strength to be evident to others, for men to see your power so they will want to join you with all urgency, you need the latest weapons."

"You have these weapons?"

Martin nodded. "In those cars I have boxes of the M1 Garand, made in the United States of America by the Winchester Repeating Arms Company. Very efficient. They fire .30-06 caliber ammunition, with eight rounds in each clip."

Ali smiled. "So. I kill you, I have guns."

"But no ammo." Martin remained unperturbed. "You are both admired and feared for your audacity and deadliness, Mahdi. So I must take precautions, so that in helping you, I do not assist you in killing me and my men."

Ali frowned.

"The cases of guns are in my cars, yes. But each box is wired with a bomb. I know how to defuse it. You do not. If you kill me, essentially you also are killing the men who try to open the booby-trapped boxes and destroying the rifles you want."

A sneer returned to Ali's face. "What do you want, infidel?"

Martin almost smiled. "Why, to help you, Ali. I want to give you guns and ammunition, but I also want to live to see many more days. So, my men and I leave your camp. With, if you wish, two or three of your trusted men. At a location upon which you and I shall agree, your men will arrive three hours later to collect the boxes of guns, from which we will have removed the explosives."

"Where will you be?"

"Gone. But you will have the guns, and with them I will leave directions to where we buried the ammunition for those guns."

"Buried?"

"Aye, two days back on our trail."

Ali shook his head, then something almost like delight changed the slant of his sneer. "You are audacious as well, infidel. You might do well to join me, I think."

"The offer is intriguing, but I am pledged to another master."

"That is well," Ali said. "For I already have a few men in my camp who imagine they might be my rivals. It is best to have only one audacious master in a band of warriors. If you stayed, I might begin to like you. And then, when I had to kill you, my heart would break."

Martin finally smiled. "I'm sure it would."

Paris

Caspar Kovacevich listened to Gregor play the piano. He smiled as he tapped the flimsy telegram paper that lay on his thigh. The news from the desert was good—in Caspar's mind, at least. Many days ago, a village had been raided by a swarm of well-armed bandits. The news informed Kovacevich that Grainger's work was progressing nicely.

He began to hum along with Gregor's playing. Caspar recalled that this particular village reportedly held an archive of ancient Islamic texts. And Casper knew a man who collected such scrolls and could be counted on to pay a fine price for them. He tapped the telegram and considered whom he might hire to travel and inquire about that archive. Someone daring enough to travel through territory now prone to violent attacks, bold enough to dicker wisely for the best items.

Just because Kovacevich would eventually possess the gold of Ophir didn't mean he planned to give up making money in the meantime.

Dakar

Roger Bernson eyed the figure standing before him with a hand extended. The fellow was brawny—Bernson could tell by the hang of his safari clothes, which clearly had never seen the bush but were still crisp from a travel trunk and, before that, an outfitting store somewhere back in civilization. The sun helmet held in the man's other hand exhibited no scuffed edges or sweat stains, so this probably was the first time it had actually been exposed to direct sunlight.

"Aye, I'm Bernson. Who are you?" He continued to ignore the offered handshake.

"Wiley Jakes," came the response, and he dropped the hand.

"Whatta you want?"

"Do you mind if I sit?" Bernson shrugged. From Jakes' voice, Bernson pegged him for a Yank.

Jakes sat across the small table from Bernson. "How about a drink?"

"I'm picky who I drink with. What do you want?"

"I'm looking for a fellow. Brendan Barnes. Disappeared into the jungle ten years ago."

"Why?"

"Why did he disappear? Or why am I looking for him?"

"Both."

"I've been assigned by his family to find him. Why he disappeared—he sought adventure in an exotic world, I think. Perhaps sitting in Boston working in the family business sounded too drab for him."

Bernson scratched his chin bristles. "How should I know how to find him? Africa's a big place."

A look of exasperation appeared, then left Jakes' face. "I say disappeared, but we know from his companions at the time where he went and where he intended to go after they parted ways. You're a guide, and a pretty good one, I hear. I need someone to lead me to where I expect to find him. You know this country, I don't. You know how to negotiate here and get where we need to go. I need your help."

"People don't say I'm a good guide because I smile a lot." He demonstrated an exaggerated grimace, revealing one black tooth among the yellowed others, minus two that had left two gaps in his dental array. "Costs money."

"I can pay."

Bernson looked over the dusty corridor that passed for a street winding among brick and mud buildings and wooden shacks with corrugated tin roofs. He let the yammering and clatter of merchants bargaining, wagons and burdened beasts groaning, and screaming children and women fill his ears. He could do the same he'd done the past several days—sit here drinking away the afternoon, find a woman for the night, wake up and start again the following morning. He'd been here too long doing nothing but waving at flies. Here was a change, come to him with no effort on his part.

"Who told you to see me?"

"Captain O'Gill."

"You came in on the *Wild Thistle*?"

Jakes nodded. Bernson waved at the one-eyed boy who worked for the owner of this place. The boy brought a jug and two tin cups, much dented but clean.

"Have a drink," Bernson offered. Jakes smiled. "Let's talk."

Jakes wiped his face with a bandana handkerchief and extended one of the cups to Bernson.

The guide laughed. "Hot doing business on the equator, hey? I happen to be free at the moment. If I do this, we'll need supplies and carriers. Depending on where this fellow is located, we may need a lot of supplies. And you'll need a holster and cartridge belt for that gun you're carrying in your pocket."

Jakes' face reddened for a moment.

"Don't worry, my friend, you'll be needing that pistol," Bernson added. "You may just need to have it handy quicker than you can pull it from your pocket. Now, where are you needing to go?"

Jakes spread over the table a map he pulled from a pocket. He pointed a route he knew Barnes had taken before separating from his companions.

"That changes things," Bernson said. "Lots of roads been built in that territory, using porters to carry materials is forbidden. Problem is, even though they have roads now, there are no cars to be had. Oh, you may find one every square five hundred or one thousand miles, but it may not run. So we'll need wagons and salted oxen. We'll still need men to hunt and probably cut trail, depending on where this Barnes ended up. You sure he's still alive?"

Jakes swabbed his face again. "That's part of what we're to determine."

"All right. And if we find him?"

Jakes shrugged. "I deliver a message. We come back."

"If we don't find him?"

Jakes shrugged again. "I'll need proof he's dead. We come back."

"Very well." Bernson swallowed the contents of his tin cup, refilled it. "This will take some money."

Jakes spread out papers from his pocket: He could draw on drafts from banks in London, Paris, and Brussels.

"That's paper. I need cash to buy what we need, for the men working for us to have confidence their families will be fed." Bernson sipped. "That bulge around your belly should mean a belt's under your shirt, and what I need is inside that belt."

Jakes frowned, then nodded.

"Very well. Expect to leave in five days."

Jakes thumped the table, spilling his cup. "That's not soon enough."

Bernson wore his poker face. "You're in Africa, my friend. It doesn't work according to the clocks in Fleet Street or New York. With the right persuasion, I may be ready in three days, but no sooner. More rush than that, we'll end up with less than the best supplies, wagons, and oxen. I don't care to encounter problems I could have avoided simply because you are in a hurry. Is that bulge in your belt big enough to make it worth the while of those people I'll need to do business with?"

"It is."

"I'll need some of that bulge to light a fire under some men. Then in three days, we'll leave."

True to his word, three days later, Bernson led Jakes and the rest of the party from the outskirts of town.

The following day, a man arrived at the same open-air bar at which Jakes had found Bernson. He was bear sized. A neatly trimmed beard of red hair covered his chin, but a vast mustache drooped from under his nose and nearly hid his mouth. He sat, wiped his face—which had turned red in the heat of walking from the dock—with a rag from his pocket, and waved to the one-eyed boy. When the youngster approached, the stranger spoke with a British accent: "I'm looking for a fellow, Roger Bernson."

The boy shook his head. "Gone. Yesterday, for the wild country."

The man shook his head. "I sent a message. My name is John Moore."

"Ah!" the boy said, then he dashed into one of the bar's dark corners and reappeared flapping a slip of paper, which he handed to Moore. "Came this morning," he explained.

Moore muttered and wadded the note, crushing it into a pea-sized knot in his palm. He peered out into the sunlight and the dust continually rising from the street—as if Bernson would appear there, hovering over the rooftops. After a few moments, he turned back to the boy. He pulled a coin from a pocket, slapped it on the table. "All right, I'll have a drink of whatever you've got that's least likely to kill me."

The boy grinned and ran to comply.

The Congo

Tchamba was now a father, and Ki-Gor and Helene had come again to visit and praise the tribe's king for the heartiness of his new son's cries and hunger.

Ki-Gor had held the child and chucked his chin, and he was ready to return home the following day. But one day's oohing and cooing was only the start of the chattering and bubbling delight Helene shared with Tchamba's many wives and the tribe's other women. Ki-Gor was itching for a fresh drama that had less feminine involvement.

The blond giant was therefore delighted in turn when NGonto and NTongo found him loitering near a stream within a short walk of Tchamba's kraal. Ki-Gor greeted the young men with great enthusiasm. "What brings you to Tchamba's tribe? Is there danger? Do I need to follow you home to fight enemies?"

The boys grinned and answered negatively. "We didn't know you were here. We came with our parents."

Ki-Gor's delight increased. "GTongo is here, too?"

"Yes," NGonto answered. "We came to see Tchamba's baby."

Ki-Gor shook his head. "And GTongo is . . ."

"Chucking the baby's chin and holding him," NTongo said, and the three chuckled together.

And so, the following day, a hunt was arranged.

The four males—Ki-Gor, GTongo, NGonto, and NTongo—set out to bring back game worthy of a royal feast. Tchamba, beginning to weary of the growing weight of feminine wisdom filling the village, wanted desperately to join the hunters, but tribal protocols required the king to stay close to his family after the birth of a son. So he handed Ki-Gor his finest spear and waved solemnly as the band jogged into the forest.

GTongo had heard that a herd of rare white deer ranged in a territory to the north. The band determined a white deer hide would make a fine gift for the royal child, so they headed that direction.

Near the end of the third day, the hunters crossed the trail of a group of men. Ki-Gor pointed to footprints—some bare, some shod. "Hunters—two, maybe three? And their porters," he said, nodding to the prints of naked feet. He examined broken leaves and stems of nearby plants and saw how the breaks did not appear fresh. "Maybe two days gone."

The tracks went off to the south.

The next day, Ki-Gor and his band crossed the trail of the same group—this time, headed north.

The fifth day, they again crossed the trail—leading west.

"These men are lost," NGonto said.

Ki-Gor showed a torn leaf to the boys' father. "Still green."

GTongo nodded. "They passed sometime today. So they are not far from here."

Ki-Gor looked at his companions, and something unspoken passed among them. Then the blond giant quickly climbed one of the towering trees nearby. High above, from one of its lower limbs, Ki-Gor launched himself into the arboreal middle terrace—a sort of rapid travelway through the trees for those nimble enough.

He followed the trail for two hours.

From the trees, Ki-Gor spotted a group of men at rest. Five were carriers sitting by or on their packs. Two were white men—one, a small, wiry fellow who appeared quite at ease, sat against the bole of a tree with his knees up, his arms out before him and resting on his knees; the other a brawny fellow, his clothing and hair disheveled, who stalked before the group and gestured widely with his arms.

Ki-Gor called down, "Hello!"

Roger Bernson jumped up from his seat by the tree. He began scouring the leafy canopy for the source of the call. Wiley Jakes, already somewhat agitated, pulled his pistol.

"I'll come down," Ki-Gor said, and moments later he stood before the guide and his client.

Jakes' eyes and mouth were open wide. The blond giant seemed to have appeared magically before him. The American raised the pistol, but Bernson grabbed his wrist and forced it down. When the guide took away his hand, Jakes rubbed the red mark—Bernson wasn't a big man, but he had a grip like iron.

"Who are you?" Bernson asked.

When Ki-Gor answered, the guide said, "I've heard of you. Third or fourth hand, anyways. Never really thought you were real, but you never know about the jungle. Monsters and mysteries." He explained their current predicament. "I hired a native guide to take us the last stretch—I know generally where we're going, but we're entering a part of the Congo I don't know so well. And situations change among tribes from time to time, so having a native guide who knew the terrain seemed like a good idea.

"From the first, he didn't seem to like the idea of where we were going. But he agreed to show us the way. Next thing you know, we get up one morning, he's gone with five of our carriers and most of our ammunition." Bernson sighed. "Wasn't like this in the old days."

"Where are you going?" Ki-Gor asked.

Bernson unfolded a map. "Here. Somewhere in this general area—between the Sangha and Lengoue Rivers—that's the last clue we have for locating Brendan Barnes."

Ki-Gor frowned. "That's difficult territory for trekking, even for locals. I know only one person who's been in that area and he had nothing good to say about it. Who is this Brendan Barnes?'

Jakes had a sour look on his face, but he spoke up: "Barnes' father is dying. He sent me to find his son, let him know about it. He wants to see the son before he kicks off."

Ki-Gor looked around at the men. "Wait here," he instructed Bernson and Jakes, then he strode to the huddled carriers. He asked some questions.

NSomu, leader of the porters, said, "We know Bernson. He is small, but like iron. His heart is strong, but is sometimes weak for money. But we will stay with him, even though we don't like this place we are going."

"You've been there?" Ki-Gor asked.

"No, but I've heard of it. I've heard it's a bad place. Not tabu, but a bad place."

The blond giant nodded before returning to the two whites.

"What if Brendan Barnes doesn't want to be found?" Ki-Gor asked.

Jakes shrugged.

Bernson said, "I've signed on to find him, so I'll look till I'm sure he can't be found."

Ki-Gor liked a challenge. "We'll find him," he said. "I'll bring up my friends. Make camp for the night here, and we'll set off in the morning." A moment more, and he was in the trees again, hurtling back to rejoin his companions.

After Ki-Gor disappeared into the leaves, Bernson directed NSomu to prepare to settle in for the night. Jakes spluttered. "You're really going to sit here and wait for that—savage—whatever it is—to come back?"

Bernson was undisturbed by Jakes' protests. "I said I'd heard of him. Everything I heard was good. If he says he'll get us where you want to go, it's worth trying."

"That guide you hired—he said he knew where he was going, and he left us here like we had a stink on our shoe."

Bernson squinted at Jakes. "I didn't have any personal dealings with that other guide. I'd heard of him second hand, from someone I trusted. Still trust. Maybe the someone I know didn't know his reference would go sour." He stopped a moment, to keep from saying something about the sourness he felt when he looked at Jakes. "If you can get where you're going without help, tell Ki-Gor when he gets back."

Bernson's client grumbled and muttered. The guide shook his head. Jakes might be a hard man on his own turf, but in the jungle's eyes, the Yank was weak. Bernson had other men as clients who were weak, and they didn't hold up -- the Congo got the best of them. But Jakes might surprise him -- being lost in unfamiliar territory, particularly a place so alien as the Congo, could upset any man.

Bernson cursed his own weakness. Taking money from men like Jakes made his work harder, but Bernson needed money. When he had it, he wasn't wise with it. But then he ended up relying on questionable characters like Jakes.

Ki-Gor reappeared with GTongo and his sons as the sun was setting.

"If you can get where you're going without help, tell Ki-Gor when he gets back."

Already it was dark in the camp, under the forest's thick canopy. NSomu's men had prepared food and set up a boma for protection from the night's dangers.

After introductions were made, the group shared a meal. GTongo kept a wary eye on Jakes, for Ki-Gor had informed his friends about his initial encounter and impressions of the travelers. Both GTongo and his sons noted that Jakes seemed twitchy and uncomfortable in the new arrivals' presence. Bernson, on the other hand, welcomed the men and clearly was an old hand at camping and working jungle trails. He didn't hide how he appreciated the help offered by Ki-Gor and his companions.

The band broke camp early and started southward. Ki-Gor and GTongo had compared notes the previous day on their march to join Bernson's camp: Ki-Gor explained Jakes' goal and stated that what he'd heard of the target territory didn't sound inviting.

"I've heard of it, too," GTongo had agreed. "My old grandfather had an old grandfather who once lived close to that country. He said it was a bad place. My old grandfather's old grandfather called it the Devil's Nest. He didn't say why it was bad, but no one wanted to go there. Ever."

The march would require many days, but GTongo already had warned his sons to be alert. Ki-Gor took to the trees and scouted far ahead of the moving party. GTongo remained in front of the group on the ground. Bernson stayed close by, a rifle slung over his shoulder, his head turning this way and that, keeping his eyes open for trouble. Jakes kept only a few yards behind, his hand close to his pistol, and the carriers followed him. NGonto and NTongo brought up the rear, ready to nock arrows to their bowstrings at a moment's notice.

Despite GTongo's concern, the party encountered nothing untoward the first two days. Camped after the second day's march, while everyone ate deer steaks from a carcass brought down by Ki-Gor on his return from scouting, the blond giant confided to GTongo away from the other's hearing: "I sent word today to Tembu George. He'll soon know what we're up to."

GTongo's eyebrows rose, a silent question.

Ki-Gor continued: "While scouting from the trees, I came across a hunting party from his tribe. Part of the reason I've been leading Bernson and Jakes this direction—I expected to encounter someone from Tembu George's kraal: they frequently hunt in this territory during this time of year."

The old warrior nodded. "They will also send word back to Helene and Tchamba?"

"Aye," Ki-Gor said. "Helene may be a bit angry, but Tchamba will be jealous that we may have an adventure without him."

Ki-Gor resumed his point position the next day when the party broke camp. His travel through the trees quickly outpaced that of his companions on the ground, so he would range forward and to the sides ahead of the group, then turn back toward them to make sure no threats had appeared between him and Bernson's crew while he prowled the territory ahead.

The jungle man was leading Bernson and the others in a southeast direction. As he moved through the middle terrace of the trees to the east, checking to see what might be coming up on that flank, Ki-Gor's keen hearing picked up an individual breathing hard as he rushed through the undergrowth. Ki-Gor moved quickly from branch to branch and spotted a small man hurrying along, frequently glancing over his back-trail. He was headed toward Ki-Gor's position, unaware that he was being watched. This stranger was unarmed but for a knife in a sheath strapped to one of his legs. A black object hung by a thong around his neck.

A crowd of men were apparently chasing the first. Ki-Gor noted that the trackers were still not close, but they followed the trail quickly.

The hunted man paused to catch his breath and look behind him. He was almost directly under Ki-Gor, who saw unfamiliar tribal scarification on the man's face and arms.

Ki-Gor dropped from his high branch to land before the stranger, who snatched his knife from its sheath as he stepped back in surprise.

"Land of Goshen! My prayers are answered. An angel from the sky!"

The man spoke in a Swahili dialect that Ki-Gor could follow. "I'm no angel. I'm a man, like you. I jumped from that tree. Why are those men chasing you?"

The man spit on the ground. "Devils are in them. They cannot stand the Word of God, so they try to kill me." He hadn't yet put away his knife, and he gave Ki-Gor a hard look. "You're not an angel. Are you really a man? Maybe you're a devil trying to kill me, too."

The blond giant smiled. "I'm a man. Come on. Your devils are getting closer." He grabbed the man, threw him over his shoulder, then made a running leap to a low branch and quickly scrambled higher into the tree, out of sight.

Perched beside Ki-Gor, the stranger gripped the branch tightly as he peered down. He'd nearly dropped his knife in shock—despite what the blond man said, surely only a devil could fly like a monkey through the trees—but he still held on to see if he might need it against this Tree Man.

Below, his pursuers came to the end of his trail. They spotted the additional set of footprints that suddenly appeared and disappeared—along with those of their quarry—with no further trail to follow. They made signs of wonder as they crouched and lifted their spears in defensive gestures. They traded frightened glances. Then, as one, they turned and dashed back the way they had come.

The worry of Ki-Gor's new companion was dispelled for a moment as he laughed deep in his belly, then he shifted his position and held the knife pointed at the blond giant. "All right, Tree Man, or Tree Devil, who are you?"

Ki-Gor smiled again. "I'm Ki-Gor. I live far from here, but I'm leading some men to a place south of here. I saw you while scouting the trail. Who are you?"

The man looked at Ki-Gor and weighed whether his explanation were some sort of trick. Finally, he answered, "I am Msoulewaki. I, too, am an alien in this place. Are you going to leave me in this tree?"

"No," Ki-Gor said. He looked at the sun through the many crossings of limbs overhead. "I'll be heading back to camp soon. You are welcome to join me."

"Is your camp in a tree?"

Ki-Gor laughed. "No, it is on the ground."

Msoulewaki nodded. "All right then. I'll go with you."

That night within the boma, while everyone relaxed after the meal, Msoulewaki related his story. He started, "I am a cannibal . . ."

"What!" Jakes had pulled his pistol when Ki-Gor translated this much.

Msoulewaki raised his palms and continued, "Do not worry. I have not eaten a man for many years." But the markings that scarred his face gave his features terrible, fierce expressions as he spoke that seemed to belie his words.

"My tribe had met a man named Cannon. He said he was a missionary, but we didn't know what that meant. He said he came to give us the Word of God. We said we already had the word of our god. We didn't need his God's word. He chuckled and said he would tell us anyway. We were glad he was a happy fellow. We told him we were going to eat him." Msoulewaki smiled and nodded.

"Nasty brutes," Jakes muttered.

"Cannon said, 'Land of Goshen! Cannibals!' He chuckled and said he was from the country of Tennessee, and people are very tough there and bad to eat. I said we had eaten a missionary before, and he wasn't hard to eat at all. When he asked who the missionary was, I showed him the book the man had left behind. The first missionary didn't chuckle like Cannon. Cannon said the book was the man's Bible, and his name was inside, Billy Rushing, and Cannon had known Billy Rushing, and he stopped chuckling and a tear came out of his eye." Msoulewaki pointed to his own eyes. "Cannon said, 'He was a great man of God.' I said, 'He was good to eat.'"

Cannon had asked the cannibal why his tribe ate people. Msoulewaki explained that they hadn't always been cannibals, but it started during tribal wars many generations ago, during the rubber wars and the revolt against the slave traders. "I told him, 'When I eat a fierce warrior, that warrior's fierceness is now mine.' Cannon said, 'Did you eat Billy Rushing?' and I said, 'Yes.' He said, 'Do you know what's in this book?' and he raised that Bible to me. I looked at him and said, 'No.'

"Cannon chuckled again. He said my eating Billy Rushing was no good, because the only thing worth anything inside Billy Rushing was the words in that Bible. 'I'm from Tennessee,' Cannon said, 'and no good to eat, and the only thing good about me is what I know, and I know what's in this Bible, but you won't get it if you eat me.'

"Well, this confused me and made me curious, so I asked Cannon to tell me about this book. So he did. And I learned I am not just a cannibal, I am a dirty sinner, but the Word of God can clean me. And it did.

"So my tribe says it's time to eat Cannon. I tell them, 'We are all dirty sinners, but Cannon can give us the Word of God, and it can clean us. So then they want to eat me, too. So I help Cannon escape, and we go find other people to tell them the Word of God, and he keeps teaching me more about the Word of God. So I'm still a sinner, but not so dirty anymore, because I believe the Word of God, and I ask the Word of God to forgive me for being a dirty sinner. And I'm not a cannibal anymore, just a sinner who knows the Word of God."

Msoulewaki showed a wide grin to the stunned faces around him in the silence that followed his tale.

"What a bunch of crap!" Jakes snarled.

Ki-Gor looked at him. "Much of the Congo is impenetrable. But I'm always surprised at how these missionaries get to some of the places they find. There are many missionary societies sending people here—some, to make up for the exploitation the Belgian government has performed; others, to exploit the feelings those activities have caused." He turned back to Msoulewaki and asked, "So that crowd chasing you today—"

"I tried to tell them about the Word of God, but they didn't like it. They had devils in them. They want to stay dirty sinners. So when they tried to kill me, I ran away. And then Ki-Gor came out of the sky and carried me away."

Bernson knew Swahili very well, thanks to his years in Africa, and hadn't needed Ki-Gor's simultaneous translation to follow Msoulewaki's story. The guide asked, "What happened to Cannon?"

The smile disappeared from the man's face. "We were in a country to the north, so many marches from here I can't count them. We were in a village. Cannon said we were going to tell these people the Word of God. The people in the village called us infidels and chased us. They killed Cannon." Tears rolled from Msoulewaki's eyes, but he smiled. "Cannon is with the Word of God now. It is what he knew best in all the world. He told me, 'I am from Tennessee, but I don't belong there. I belong with the Word of God.' And that is where he is."

Wiley Jakes gave a shout the next morning after he arose and saw that Msoulewaki was missing.

Ki-Gor spoke up. "He left during the night."

Jakes spluttered, "He's some sort of spy. Wants to lead his cannibal friends here to attack us and gnaw our bones."

"No," the blond giant reassured him. "When he learned we are going south, he wanted to return north. He told me when he left that he believes his work is to continue Cannon's efforts with the tribes north of here."

Jakes grumbled and went off to prepare for the day's travel. Bernson appeared unfazed—just as he had during Msoulewaki's recitation the previous night. The guide had heard and seen so many extraordinary things that little surprised him now. Still, his gaze lingered on Ki-Gor a few moments, as if suspecting the jungle man of withholding some details about the evangelistic cannibal's exit.

Indeed, Ki-Gor had told Jakes only a partial truth.

As the camp prepared to bed down for the night, Ki-Gor had observed Msoulewaki go to his knees, knit his hands together, then bend down to put his forehead against the earth and pray silently. He'd also noted Jakes' skeptical expression when the American had glanced toward the newcomer.

During the night, Ki-Gor's jungle-trained senses had awakened him when Msoulewaki crept out of the boma. The blond giant's mighty thews carried him over the barrier with a single leap; he quickly caught up to Msoulewaki. The reformed cannibal wasn't hurrying away, as though escaping, but was walking slowly through the forest during the night, heading north. Ki-Gor confronted the man:

"Where do you go, Msoulewaki?"

The man was startled to learn that he'd been discovered. "Tree Man, you move so quiet—are you sure you aren't an angel? Land of Goshen, when I heard your voice, I nearly jumped high enough to be a tree man like you.

"I'm going back to where Cannon was working. His work is my work now. This is the last thing he gave me," he said as he lifted the black object from around his neck—a compass. "I use it to go north. It is like the Word of God, Cannon said. It shows me the way to go so I won't get lost."

He looked closely at Ki-Gor, and the jungle man could see that Msoulewaki was weighing whether to say more. Finally, he continued: "The Wiley Jakes man does not like me. He is afraid I will gobble him up. He thinks I lie, that I am still a dirty sinner cannibal. I think that is because he is still a dirty sinner and he lies himself. He did not like when you and Iron Man Bernson told me where you are traveling. He is afraid of something. Being eaten, yes, but something else I do not know."

Msoulewaki took a bearing with his compass before returning it to hang from his neck. "And I do not want to go south. I want to go back to my work for Cannon and for the Word of God. South is bad. When you told me about where you are going, I remember I have heard about it. It is called the Devil's Nest. I go to the north, where the devils are nested in men's hearts and minds, but the Word of God can shake them clean. But that Devil's Nest in the south—" He shrugged, made a gesture of farewell to Ki-Gor, and resumed his trek northward.

When the party resumed its trek, Bernson remained at the front with GTongo, alert and wary, while Ki-Gor roamed ahead. Wiley Jakes frequently looked behind, as if an attack by Msoulewaki and a horde of hungry cannibals with filed teeth was imminent. His hand didn't stray far from the handle of his pistol. For hours at a time, he carried it unholstered, his finger on the trigger.

So the march continued. On the afternoon of the fifth day after Msoule-waki left the camp, the party stopped: GTongo and Bernson came upon Ki-Gor sitting in the middle of the elephant trail the group had been following. The trail angled to the left. It turned at the spot on which Ki-Gor sat—before a wall of bright green. The wall was a barrier of plants, from eight to sixteen feet tall, and so dense a man could not shove his way through nor push even an arm into the mass. The plants varied—some were tall grasses with thick blades, others were long-stemmed varieties with wide, shovel-shaped leaves.

Bernson asked, "Can we get around?"

Ki-Gor shook his head. "It's the biggest plant brake I've ever encountered." He pointed to the trail. "Even the elephants can't beat it. Come with me." He walked back a few yards to the nearest tall tree, then directed Bernson to climb onto his back piggy-back style. Then the blond giant scrambled up the trunk of the tree with his rider. Bernson felt unmanly being carried in this way, but he marveled at Ki-Gor's tremendous strength and agility. The jungle man stopped on a thick branch twenty feet in the air. "Look."

Bernson gazed out over a sea of green that stretched, seemingly, to the horizon. No trees interrupted the bright foliage—the plants grew so tightly together, no tree seedling had a hope of surviving in that mass. "Good Lord."

Ki-Gor said, "According to the directions you received and your maps, that's where we must go. Perhaps this vast brake is why men call the area the Devil's Nest—or perhaps there is something evil beyond."

"How do we continue?"

"If Jakes wants to go on, the only way is to cut a trail."

Back on the ground, Bernson told Jakes and the others what he'd seen. His client's eyes twitched, and he glared at the tangle that blocked their way. His fingers and knuckles gripping his gun turned white. For a moment, Bernson thought the man might raise his pistol and fire at the brake as if bullets would solve the problem. Then Jakes turned his reddened eyes on the guide and said, "Let's go on."

Ki-Gor and NSomu took up the machetes that had been used as needed to cut trail on the way. Each gave the other a solemn look, nodded, then set upon the wall of green, chopping at the stems and leaves as though hacking through a squad of enemy warriors.

After an hour, the two had cut a narrow track about ninety feet into the brake. Two of the carriers took over, and an hour later the track had been extended another sixty feet.

The next morning, cutting started before sunrise. By mid-afternoon they came across a sump, which allowed them to replenish their water supply. Bernson called a halt at dusk, when another hour was spent to clear enough space for tents and a cookfire. Then everyone sat, exhausted, ate, and fell twitching and dreamless into sleep.

So it went, morning until dark.

After ten days, the party had made only a little more than two miles into the barrier. Although a thin strip of sky was visible directly overhead, the sensation was similar to living in a tunnel of surrounding greenness.

The men's humor was grim. On the eleventh day, Bernson said, "I don't know if this really is the Devil's Nest, but it sure looks like some ring of Hell to me."

"How about that?"

So said Billy McShane, the Yank who had come through more than one scrape with Martin Grainger to benefit Caspar Kovacevich's personal treasury.

Five days past, he'd sat on a branch of a tree, high above the ground, peering through field glasses at the narrow trail hacked out of the leafy brake by Bernson's party. He'd gotten a rough count of the party, but continued to watch, fascinated at the men's struggle against the green barrier.

Billy had managed to climb to his perch by linking together the leather belts from each man of Grainger's crew, fastening the loop around the tree and his own backside with some slack, and shimmying up the trunk like a logger in the North American forests.

Grainger and his men had trekked through the jungle from where they had abandoned their vehicles far north from here. When they reached the green brake, they began walking its perimeter to find some trail through the barrier and came across the signs of a recent slashing into the leafy mass.

Billy finally came down in response to Grainger's call and reported what he'd seen. "Do you think they're on the way to Ophir, too?"

Grainger stared at the break in the barrier before speaking. "That would suggest a leak of information from Caspar—and he holds his information tightly, so that's not likely. However, they're going the same direction as we

...he'd sat on a branch, high above the ground, peering through field glasses...

are. Perhaps Caspar has more than one group of men heading to Ophir, to cover his bets. That also seems unlikely, knowing Caspar, and your description of the crew doesn't sound like a force to be reckoned with, as our own is. Still, the coincidence is remarkable and hard to ignore."

Billy, rash in many ways—deadly in all—scuffed his boot toe in the dirt. "Do we join them? Kill them? What?"

Grainger looked at the sky. "We'll back off from this opening. Camp for the night. They're going our way—we'll let them keep working. Tire themselves out, if necessary, while we rest and plan."

Billy scoffed. "Rest and plan?"

Grainger understood the need for continual movement that flowed through Billy's blood. It fueled the violence that could explode so suddenly from the American, so Grainger aimed that violence to make it effective— like artillery pointed toward an enemy instead of like a grenade blowing up in the middle of one's own men. Although he had kept his men active and moving for weeks, he was prepared for enforced downtime. Grainger pulled an object from his pack and tossed it to Billy, whose lightning-like reflexes kicked in so the Yank snagged it one-handed.

Billy looked at it. "A baseball?"

"I know you hate to sit still," Grainger said. "That will keep you moving while you sit. While those fellows ahead clear the way and wear down." He nodded and smiled. "Then we'll move forward."

The men had been slashing through the green brake for two weeks. They looked like prisoners who'd been on forced marches. The wrappings on their hands were stained with the blood that seeped from their palms. Their faces, shaggy with unkempt beards, had a haunted look.

Hacking a way through the foliage had become a sort of obsession. Giving up and turning back seemed more impossible than continuing the mindless cutting, step after step.

Ki-Gor looked at them all as they hunkered over their food, eating without tasting, without speaking. The American's face appeared inflamed, his eyes those of a man going mad. The jungle man glanced at Bernson, who looked surreptitiously at Jakes. Ki-Gor knew the guide wanted to warn him that Jakes soon would crack, but there had been no opportunities for anyone to speak privately with another. In this case, there was no need— Ki-Gor could read the signs of Jakes' coming collapse as well as Bernson could track game on safari.

The meal completed, Ki-Gor walked back about fifty yards along the green tunnel to sit as night watch, as he had done every night since the tunneling had begun. The only way a threat could reach them would be by following the trail the expedition members had cut.

They began again the next morning. Three hours into the day's work of hacking through the green, Ki-Gor stopped. He turned slowly, gazing into the strip of blue overhead.

Bernson noticed. "Do you hear something?" he asked.

Jakes swore. "It's just the bugs. They never stop screeching. Or the wind in the top of the grass. Bugs and wind and grass. That's it. That's what he hears! Bugs and wind and grass!"

"No," Ki-Gor answered. "Something else. Coming through the sky."

The guide looked bewildered. "The sky? Are you sure?" Bernson craned his neck. He knew Jakes was nearly over the edge. Maybe all of them were, even Ki-Gor, although the jungle man's stamina and strength seemed ever unflagging.

"There."

Ki-Gor said the word calmly, but Bernson felt a trill of excitement fly through his limbs as he first perceived the low-pitched thrumming that steadily increased. Then the source came into sight as it entered the narrow strip of visibility from the tunnel: a dirigible.

Their shouts were like those of men seeing a ship after being marooned on an island for months.

All except for Ki-Gor. He frowned as he peered up at the airship. Would it mean rescue, or captivity?

Msoulewaki was running. Again.

His compass no longer hung from his neck. It was gone, lost. But for now, Msoulewaki didn't care which direction he traveled. From the sounds of bodies crashing through the brush behind him—the angry yells, threats, and deprecations—the entire tribe was chasing him. Perhaps a neighboring tribe or two, as well.

Land of Goshen, Msoulewaki thought between gasps for air as he dashed among branches and clawing vines, *the devils in these people's skulls are particularly evil and persistent. Perhaps the Word of God needs an assistant. The Cudgel of God.*

He splashed through a shallow stream, praying that no swimming snakes might be nearby.

He clambered over massive deadfalls. Crawled under low-hanging branches.

Yes, Cudgel of God. Crack open the skulls, let the light of day and the Gospel shine in on those devils, burn them to a crisp.

The pursuers were getting closer, their clamoring louder and—if possible—more violent.

The undergrowth was thinning, impeding Msoulewaki's headlong flight less with each step. Then he burst through a tangle of thick vines to emerge into a vast clearing, perhaps two miles wide.

Easier running, Msoulewaki thought, *but if any of those devils have a throwing arm worth having, I'll soon have a spear through my guts.*

He took a deep breath, resumed running—headed for the trees at the other side of the grassy clearing.

The voices were louder, and he glanced back to see the first of the tribesmen breaking out of the forest and racing into the low grass. He saw spears being cocked back over shoulders.

Msoulewaki kept running, gasping, and prayed to the Word of God: "Dear Lord, please save me from these devils."

That's when he heard a strange thrumming he hadn't noticed earlier. A low, down-in-the-belly sort of noise. Over the grasses swam a wide darkness, a shadow that crossed the ground swiftly, moving in a line that would quickly intersect with Msoulewaki's path.

The man, already frightened for his life, was near frenzy as he watched the shadow's progress along the ground. Then he looked up.

He stopped running. His mouth opened. His eyes widened.

Overhead. In the sky.

Msoulewaki's voice was a panting whisper: "Land of Goshen. The Pillar of Cloud."

The Pillar of Cloud accompanied Moses and the children of Israel after they left behind slavery in Egypt and Pharoah's army drowned in the Red Sea. But if what Msoulewaki now saw was a pillar, it had toppled, for it did not stand vertically, but lay horizontally in the sky. Light flashed from its sides in glaring bursts that left spots floating in the hunted man's vision.

His pursuers had stopped in a close-gathered body, pointing at the strange apparition in the sky, their spears ready to fly.

The thrumming sound from the pillar had changed, and now it sat still in the air, directly overhead. Another sound issued from above, a voice.

Msoulewaki couldn't make out the words, but his legs nearly went out from under him.

Then he noticed that a portion of pillar had detached itself from the cloud's belly and was descending straight toward the ground. Seeing this, Msoulewaki fell back onto the grasses, unable to take his gaze from the lowering section—which halted about ten feet above him.

The section of cloud was actually a sort of platform with a cage marking its sides. Three men peered out at him—one was taller and wider than the other two, and his head and face were covered with hair like burnished copper. Msoulewaki cried out, "Are you angels?"

The red-haired man laughed. "Thank goodness you speak some sort of Swahili. No, not angels. Close, however—we're British! Do you need help?"

Msoulewaki noticed now the rifles held by the other two men. They were aimed toward the huddled tribesmen many yards back. The group cowered, but still called out threats.

Msoulewaki returned to his feet. "You are not angels, and you do not ride in the Pillar of Cloud?"

The big man scratched his red beard. "Pillar of Cloud? Oh," and he laughed again, "no, this is a dirigible. A number were left about after the War wanting some use. The Royal Geographical Society latched onto this one. Dirigible—air ship. This landing platform lowers and rises with mechanical winches aboard the gondola up there—makes boarding and disembarking much easier in places there is no mooring mast. Do you want to come aboard?"

Msoulewaki looked at the flashing skin of the aircraft and thought of the prophet Elijah, carried into the sky by a flaming chariot. He turned and looked at the raised spears of his pursuers. Then he spoke to the men in the floating cage. "Yes, thank you."

The red-haired giant opened a hinged door in the side of the cage and dropped down a rope ladder. One of the armed men said, "Doctor, the captain won't—"

The man with the mustache and beard interrupted: "Never mind the captain, son. I'll speak with him."

Msoulewaki wasted no time climbing aboard. One of the armed men moved a lever, and the platform began to rise, pulled up by the thick cables attached to its corners. He looked over the edge and as he retreated from the ground saw the irate tribesmen begin to scatter back toward the trees—they wanted nothing more to do with this stranger who spoke about the Word of God and allowed himself to be swallowed by some flying behemoth.

Msoulewaki looked up at the hole in the shadowed belly of the dirigible—a house that could carry men and fly like a cloud. "Land of Goshen! The world is full of wonders." He looked at the bearded man and saw humor and confidence in his face. Msoulewaki introduced himself, extending his hand as Cannon had taught him. The big man shook his hand and said, "A pleasure to meet you. I'm John Moore. Welcome to the *Pegasus*."

The *Pegasus*, after spotting Ki-Gor, Bernson and the others, moved into position and lowered its platform. The men on the ground were quite surprised to see Msoulewaki among those approaching from the sky.

A rope ladder dropped and unrolled from the platform. Msoulewaki and a bearish man with red hair clambered down. Ki-Gor saw that two men armed with rifles remained on the platform.

The reformed cannibal introduced John Moore, and the two men recounted their initial encounter.

"Msoulewaki learned I was heading this direction, and told me about your party," Moore said. "We kept a lookout for you—never imagining your trail through this vast green sea would be so visible from the air. We can easily provide transport over this dense barrier—and you can rest on the way."

Jakes barked from a few yards away, his gun in hand. "And you, Moore—where are you going?" He looked feverish, like a man falling into a nightmare.

Moore's eyebrows went up. "I work for the Royal Geographic Society. And occasionally the British Museum, or at times—like the present—for both simultaneously. My patrons have sent me forth to find something."

"What is it?" demanded Jakes. "What are you looking for?"

Moore smiled. "I must unfortunately be so impolite as to refuse to answer. My business for the Society requires some—ah, care, I suppose is the word—care in how public its information may be shared."

Ki-Gor watched the two men, Moore and Jakes. Although the man from the clouds appeared jovial and utterly sincere, the jungle man's honed senses could tell that Moore was not sharing complete truths with them. And Jakes—whose motives Ki-Gor had doubted from the first—appeared more brittle every second. The blond giant's weight shifted as he prepared to leap onto the American if he raised his gun to shoot.

Moore continued: "My mission, however, doesn't prevent me from offering you gentlemen a ride to your destination, or at least past this barrier, if you prefer. I assure you our sky-riding craft has been fitted with every convenience you'll find on a sea-going passenger vessel, and you'll be quite comfortable. And surely more refreshed by journey's end."

Bernson spoke up. "We'll accept your offer, Mr. Moore."

"Doctor," Moore interrupted.

"Dr. Moore, then," Bernson said. "We need rest from this green hell. And it's come none too soon." He looked at Jakes, who seemed suddenly catatonic. The guide reached toward his client, and Jakes put up no fuss as Bernson slipped the revolver from his hand. He led the American to the rope ladder and helped him ascend. While NSomu and his men and the supplies went up, Moore shook Ki-Gor's hand.

"Msoulewaki told me of your prowess," he said. "We'll be glad to have you aboard. These are your friends?" Moore gestured to GTongo, NGonto, and NTongo.

Ki-Gor introduced them all. "We are lucky you arrived," the jungle man said.

"Luck?" Moore smiled. "Msoulewaki might say—in a different manner, of course—that the hand of Providence stirs every pot, Mr. Ki-Gor. I've heard of you—rumors and hints—and I'm glad to see you're quite real. I suspect you are quite the adventurer. We may be very alike in that manner. I should enjoy hearing your tales."

"But you will not share with us your story of what brings you here?" Ki-Gor asked.

Moore's smile turned a bit grim. "I fear I may not. But perhaps we shall be fortunate enough to share an adventure?" He strode to the rope.

Msoulewaki clapped Ki-Gor on the shoulder and urged him to the ladder. "Come, my Tree Man friend. It is time for you, like me, to become a Cloud Climber."

"The devil."

Billy McShane peered through his field glasses as the *Pegasus*—its platform now returned to the belly of the gondola—began to increase its altitude and move farther to the south.

While Ki-Gor, Bernson and the rest had slashed through the foliage, Billy had impatiently paced, played catch by bouncing a baseball against the wide trunk of a tree, and frequently climbed to this limb to review the cutters' progress. He watched a while longer, then scampered to the ground from his tree-branch perch. He reported to Grainger everything he'd observed. "How do we get through this mess now?" Billy demanded. "That crew didn't finish cutting a trail through this overgrown garden—do we march over their trail and take it up?"

Martin Grainger remained patient in the face of the Yank's exasperation. "That's one way through. I think Juri has found another."

While his band had camped and rested, Grainger had sent some of his men scouting along the perimeter of the vast brake in search of other passage through or around the natural barrier. Juri Lindroos had encountered, miles from the camp, an outcropping of rock that appeared quite anomalous from its surroundings. Further investigation turned up a well-hidden opening—an entrance to a rough-hewn tunnel. It was small—Lindroos and his companions had to hunker down a bit to keep their heads clear of the ceiling—but clear, as though it were maintained or used with at least some regularity. Over the course of several days, Lindroos had explored about five miles of the main tunnel and its branches. He had reported to Grainger his belief that the tunnel would provide a way past the wall of foliage.

"But we don't know yet," Grainger concluded his explanation to Billy and the others. "So we'll divide into two groups. Billy, pick four others— you'll take up hacking the brush where those others left off." He ignored the ugly grimace that appeared on McShane's face—Grainger understood that Billy had been idle too long, and needed to expend some restless energy swinging a machete. "The rest of us will tackle Juri's tunnel. If we come through to the other side quickly, I'll send Tommy back for you to join us through the passage. If you break clear before Tommy comes to you, sit tight on the other side of the brake for a day. If we don't connect up, send one of your men back through your cleared trail to the tunnel mouth for us. Understood?"

Billy kept his jaws clamped tight, squeezed the baseball until his knuckles turned white, then nodded.

Grainger didn't even nod in reply. "All right then. Let's go."

Ki-Gor wasn't accustomed to such luxury as the *Pegasus* offered its passengers and crew, but he appreciated the amazing view from the gondola's ports. The jungle stretched out below and beyond from a vantage the blond giant had never imagined.

The captain of the airship barely restrained his contempt for his passengers, but he acceded to John Moore's authority as leader for the expedition. Ki-Gor didn't completely ignore the captain's rebuffs, but he remained wary of Moore's intentions.

Jakes had collapsed into a seeming coma as soon as the entire party had boarded the *Pegasus*. Twelve hours later, he had appeared from his cabin clean, shaved, and much restored. Like Ki-Gor, he didn't seem to trust Moore, but he was far more obvious in expressing his distrust. He rarely spoke unless asked a direct question, and he looked at men from the corners of his eyes.

GTongo, NGonto, and NTongo stood with Ki-Gor and peered through the observation port. The father and two sons clutched their bows and kept a quiver of arrows slung from a shoulder. "It does not feel right to have this false floor beneath my feet," GTongo said. "The ground is the ground. I know where I am when I stand on it. This cloud ground moves around—it is in a different place when I wake up in the morning."

Ki-Gor smiled. "If not for this airship, the ground beneath our feet would still be covered by that thick growth we were hacking through."

GTongo grunted, noncommittal, while his sons attempted to restrain their grins. Unlike their father, NGonto and NTongo were thrilled by this ride.

The group was joined by Dr. Moore, Roger Bernson, and Msoulewaki. Wiley Jakes drifted in as well, but remained a bit apart from the other men. Ki-Gor knew Moore was entering as soon as the bulkhead door opened-- his wilderness-honed senses detected the scent that the Briton wore. The jungle man had noticed it emanating from Moore at their first meeting, and recognized it as a vestige of a fragrance he'd detected from Wiley Jakes. The scent overwhelmed any other scent that might otherwise have been noticed by Ki-Gor's sensitive nose—which the jungle man found very disconcerting, because he relied on his keen sense of smell to warn him of dangers not yet within sight, but brought to his attention by wandering winds.

He'd asked Bernson about this smell the men from civilization wore. The guide had laughed, called it bay rum, and explained that men applied the liquid to seem desirable to women.

"They want to find mates here in the Congo?" Ki-Gor had asked.

Bernson laughed again. "No, no, but men wear this scent to appear manly."

The jungle man's face apparently exhibited a funny expression, because the guide nearly laughed aloud again.

Ki-Gor would have to ask Helene if she found his strong personal odor an attraction.

Otherwise, Ki-Gor considered the fragrance another method of hiding the truth—he was convinced Moore was not sharing all the truth about his trip to the jungle. And so Ki-Gor didn't completely trust the man.

While the others greeted one another, Jakes kept silent. Moore wore a comfortable traveling suit, and Bernson and Jakes wore cleaned safari gear; the difference was striking between these men and the jungle-born men, who still wore the animal hides that served as their loin cloths. This functional apparel certainly distinguished Msouliwake, Ki-Gor and his friends from the crisp and creased crew handling the airship, and only Moore's presence restrained the captain from openly sneering at his passengers when situations forced him to join their company.

One of the craft's uniformed men entered through a door that provided entrance to the ship's bridge. "Dr. Moore," he said, "we've spotted some activity below."

"Excellent!" Moore answered. "Have the captain lower the ship, and we'll get a look."

The newcomer exited, and moments later the men gathered at the port noticed the ship slanting earthward.

"There!" Ngonto pointed. "I see them!"

GTongo uttered another grunt. Msoulewaki squinted. "What are they doing?"

Moore frowned. "Cricket? Are they really playing cricket?"

Jakes surprised them all when he guffawed, a look of incredulous delight on his face. "They're playing baseball!"

The men pushed their noses closer to the glass of the port, trying to make out details. They saw a group of black-skinned people arranged in a particular order—some rushing after a small ball, one running pell-mell from spot to spot.

Ki-Gor was fascinated. "What's baseball?"

Before an answer was supplied, Msoulewaki shouted, "Look out!"

He pointed. From the floor of the jungle came hurtling toward the airship a large bundle of flame, followed by a second and third.

The deck seemed to lurch underfoot as the crew, alert in the bridge, shifted the airship's flight to evade the missiles. The effort appeared unnec-

The second salvo also passed harmlessly below the Pegasus.

essary, however, for the trajectory of the balls of fire peaked and began arc-
ing groundward before reaching the craft's height. But as the three fireballs
began their descent, three more missiles appeared—flying upward from a
clearing of the jungle floor.

This second salvo also passed harmlessly below the *Pegasus*. No subsequent threats rose from the forest. Jakes, still peering at the ground, said,
"There's a white man down there!"

Bernson said, "I see him. He's waving to us."

"They're all waving now," Ki-Gor added.

"It's Barnes," Jakes said, and Moore turned a sharp look at the American,
who repeated, "It's Barnes."

Ki-Gor, GTongo and his sons walked through tall grass toward a stand
of trees. Msoulewaki and Bernson followed a few yards behind, with
Moore, Jakes, and two armed crewman bringing up the rear. The pilot of
the *Pegasus* had located a clearing two miles from where Barnes had been
sighted, and the party had been landed on the retracting platform at that
point. NSomu and the other carriers also had been landed, because they
distrusted flying through the air. They remained behind, near the airship,
weapons at the ready should the contact party return in a hurry.

Ki-Gor and his friends led the others into the trees to meet the men
they had spotted from the sky.

Ki-Gor's eyes and nose still smarted from the aftershave worn by Moore
and Jakes. Even though they were several yards away, the man-made scent
blunted the jungle-trained senses of the blond giant. So much so that he
didn't detect the men in the group coming through the trees before he
spotted them coming out of the shadows.

They move silently through the foliage, he thought. *They are surely formidable warriors.*

The two parties met. The strangers were small men, pygmies like Ki-
Gor's friend, N'Geeso, although even smaller in stature. Still, they bristled
with weapons—spears, bows and arrows, long-bladed knives—and their
faces were painted with frightful designs to create a fierce expression to
send fear into the hearts of less-mighty fighters.

Ki-Gor and the strangers both advanced with their hands raised, palms
forward, in a non-threatening demonstration. The pygmy in the lead—he
was followed by ten others—spoke first. Ki-Gor was surprised to hear a

dialect of isiZulu or Bantu: "You are white like the Uncle! More marvels! A flying hippopotamus the Uncle says carries friends, and the friends it carries are white like the Uncle."

For several minutes the two groups introduced themselves, because the etiquette of jungle folk follows extensive formal rules. Eventually, the pygmies turned and began to lead their new acquaintances back to their village.

Jakes, who understood Bantu as well as he knew Chinese, asked Bernson, who had been translating for the American, "What about this Uncle? Is that Barnes?"

The guide shrugged. "They never said a name. Maybe they don't know his name. Maybe *Uncle* is all they know. We'll find out when we get there."

"Do you think it's a trap?"

Bernson saw sweat leaking from Jakes' hat band, saw the Yank's gaze darting into the shadows of the surrounding trees and vines. "Why trap us when they could have killed us already? There are probably thirty or forty more of them hidden around us, out of sight."

Jakes' eyes widened, and he wrapped his palm around the butt of his pistol.

Bernson smiled grimly, then strode up to join Ki-Gor.

The pygmies led the band of travelers to a large kraal. They were met by a crowd of curious pygmy men and women and chattering children. The latter shouted, "Uncle! Uncle!" as they laughed and pointed at the white men.

From one of the huts, its doorway was taller than that of the other structures, stepped a slender white man dressed in a canvas jacket over a vest, collarless shirt, jodhpurs and well-tended boots. A yellow kerchief was tied loosely around his throat. His long ginger hair flew wildly around his head in the breeze, but his mustache and beard were neatly trimmed.

He looked frail, but his grip was strong when he shook hands with Ki-Gor. "Welcome, welcome to our home. My name is Brendan Barnes."

Ki-Gor quickly glanced at Jakes and saw that Bernson and Moore had done the same. The American looked calmer than he had in days. His hand no longer appeared ready to clutch and pull his sidearm.

Ki-Gor introduced the entire party. He noted that Jakes demonstrated no more enthusiasm or anxiety in greeting Barnes than did the other newcomers.

Barnes escorted the visitors to an open-air gathering of the tribe to share food and drink. Once everyone else was seated and served, a group of the pygmies brought a large woven cushion more colorfully dyed than any others for Barnes to sit upon. After Barnes was settled, a still larger cushion, covered with a flawless white hide, was brought out and placed beside the white man. Then the pygmies situated around the food shouted, "Uncle!"

Barnes bowed, then smiled, and the meal began.

Ki-Gor had followed the preparations closely. The tribesmen clearly loved and respected Barnes, but did not offer him the sort of obeisance typically given a king or other tribal leader.

Barnes offered explanations while everyone ate. "These are the Kkorch-be, which is not a Swahili or Zulu or Bantu word, but from my best guess is a word older even than those languages. It means 'The People', not an unusual declaration for a folk and their identity. I found them, or they found me, a few years ago. I must admit I was looking for them", he smiled again, "without really knowing I was doing so."

Moore asked, "What brought you here?"

"My family had for many years been associated with the Jellyby Foundation in London. As supporters, we regularly received reports of the Foundation's work in Borrioboola-Gha and elsewhere in Africa. I found a stash of these reports when I was a boy and devoured them. I was thereafter utterly fascinated by the mysteries and tribes of Africa. So, my studies completed as a young man, I made my way here to learn more, face to face." He shrugged. "Much against the desires of my family, I must say. Supporting with the hands, feet, and mind is quite another thing than writing a periodic bank draft."

A child ran to Barnes and leaped into his lap. He laughed and fed him from his bowl.

"Once I was in the country, I wandered about, attaching myself to various expeditions and study groups. I heard about a particularly aggressive tribe of warriors in a remote region. They raided and attacked. They were so fierce, none of the other tribes in that country could retaliate successfully. So I trekked and questioned, slowly finding my way through the Congo, tenderfoot's luck, I must say, in many instances, although I was in a terrible state toward the end of my journey. Sick, near delirious, dehydrated, probably quite near death, to be honest. But I was found by the Kkorchbe, the very people I was looking for. They tended to me, got me back on my feet, and I've been here with them since."

Bernson looked puzzled as he gazed around the happy pygmy faces surrounding them.

"These are the warlike people you heard about?" he asked.

Barnes chuckled. "Yes. Great warriors. They dominated the entire region. Frightened all their neighbors into submission. Not to rule them, just to attack for earning honor and capturing booty. Something similar to the American Indian tribes, who raided one another for counting coup and capturing horses, weapons, and so on."

Bernson shook his head. "Don't look so fierce at the moment."

"I've been able to re-channel some of those aggressive tendencies," Barnes explained.

"And because of that, I must apologize for endangering your air vehicle," he added, "which I so hope you will allow me to visit."

"I fear I'm a bit lost," Moore said.

"Yes, I'm sorry," Barnes continued. "Once I was up and around, I convinced the Kkorchbe that they were such great warriors, well, they'd proven it to everyone in the country. I'd even heard about their prowess in lands far marches from here. Really, there was no need to continue making war on other tribes. Instead, they could focus on developing ways to defend their country from enemies foolish enough to attack."

"Oh?" Moore clearly was genuinely interested in how a single man, an outsider, had diverted an entire tribe's cultural tradition.

Barnes nodded. "I'm sure you encountered the Wall of Grasses, a natural barrier sure to thwart most attempted incursions. The Kkorchbe have a few well-hidden tunnels under the Wall, they used them for their excursions to make war on the surrounding countryside. But everything they need, really, is here in their own country."

Moore interrupted. "You were, ah, apologizing for attacking the *Pegasus*?"

"The *Pegasus,* what a wonderful name for your ship! Yes, I'm sorry, I was getting carried away." Barnes lifted the child from his lap, sent him off to his mother. "The Kkorchbe have demonstrated a marked facility for mechanics. One wouldn't immediately suspect this, because of their reliance on spears, knives, and bows and arrows. But as a defensive measure, I led them in building a trebuchet."

"A what?" Jakes demanded.

"A catapult," Moore said, more as an aside than as an actual response to the American, for his attention was keenly focused on Barnes.

"Indeed," said their host. "The Kkorchbe were quite taken with its destructive properties, and they've become rather competitive in constructing more of these engines with longer ranges and increased load capacities."

Bernson rubbed his chin. "So those flaming missiles that attacked the *Pegasus*..."

"Yes, I'm afraid the tribe saw your ship as a threat and used their armaments to defend their homes. My apologies, as I said. Once I saw the British markings, I calmed their fears and ended the bombardment."

The meal was ended. When Barnes stood, the crowd again shouted, "Uncle!" and his cushion was whisked away, along with the white cushion on which no one had sat.

"What's this 'Uncle' stuff?" Jakes asked.

Barnes offered another of his disarming smiles. "For some reason, perhaps because of my white skin, or perhaps there's more than that, the Kkorchbe frequently made reference to some story or legend or prophecy when I first arrived, and I've yet to get the whole thing straight, even after all this time, anyway, they tried to make me their ruler, a king. I refused. Staunch believer in American democracy, you know. The Kkorchbe have no king, just a sort of council of elders. I fended off their attempts, and finally settled on being what I called an uncle, sort of an advisor, I guess you'd say. No being a ruler for me, thank you very much.

"So, from my uncle-ing, I've reduced their warfare and introduced some Western medieval engineering."

Moore frowned. "And the unused white cushion?"

"Ah," Barnes said. "That seat is reserved for the warlord. And except in times of war, there is no warlord. One is appointed only when attacking or defending. So the white seat remains empty, these days."

"But surely," Moore disputed, "you can't have altered their entire culture so completely in such a short time, from so warlike a lifestyle. Look, even the competition in building war machines can't be enough to satisfy a cultural imperative that existed for, well, who knows how long."

Barnes rubbed his hands together with a vigor clearly arising from delight. "Quite right. Come along."

He led them to a clearing outside the kraal. The grasses here were cut low, and a rough square was marked with four small pillows or bags. Near the center of the square was a raised mound, clear of grass.

NGonto leaned toward Ki-Gor and whispered, "What is it? A field for sacrifice?" The blond giant shrugged.

Jakes shouted, "Baseball! I was right!"

Ki-Gor had watched the American closely the entire while, and now there showed in his face a great delight at finally encountering something familiar.

"Yes, Mr. Jakes, baseball," Barnes replied. "The competitiveness of the Kkorchbe truly thrives in mastering the grace and fury of the great American pastime."

Moore looked skeptical. "Why not cricket?"

Jakes asked, "What about balls and bats?" Talking about baseball seemed to have given the suspicious American more comfort even than the *Pegasus'* amenities, Ki-Gor thought.

Barnes laughed. "The Kkorchbe are artisans in making their tools and weapons. They show as much care in crafting a glove and ball and bat from animal hides, gut, and local hardwoods."

Ki-Gor turned to Barnes. "What is baseball?"

Their host's eyes almost seemed to twinkle. He shouted out, "Warm ups!" and the pygmies who had crowded around the visitors abruptly dashed over to positions around the diamond. Gloves were pulled on, and the men began hurling a ball to one another with seemingly mere flicks of their wrists. A solid SMACK sounded from each glove, to Jakes' eyes quite different from the cowhide versions from home, but apparently well-made by the jungle craftsmen, just the same.

Another tribesman picked up an odd-shaped bat and began to launch fly balls to players in the outfield, Whack-Whack!

Moore pointed to the batter. "Is that fellow abusing a cricket bat?"

Barnes corrected him. "A fungo bat, Dr. Moore. Quite a specialized piece of equipment."

GTongo and his sons laughed and shouted encouragement during the exercises, while Msoulewaki peered over Ki-Gor's shoulder, somewhat fearful that one of those hurled or hit balls would veer from its intended course toward his unprotected head.

Bernson watched the display of the Kkorchbe's prowess and shook his head. Small black men wearing paint and loin covers, playing an American game taught by a cracked, rich Yankee. "I must be drunk back in Dakar," he thought.

The demonstration complete, the Kkorchbe trotted off the field as Jakes clapped and stomped in approval.

The crowd returned to the kraal. Barnes walked near the rear of the group with his guests. "Now my new friends," he asked, "what brings you to our small part of the world?"

"One reason, that we know of," Bernson said, and he looked at Dr. Moore before gesturing to Jakes. "My client hired me to find you, Mr. Barnes. Mr. Jakes can explain why."

Jakes cleared his throat and patted his pockets, as if searching for notes. "Mr. Barnes, I was hired to tell you your father is dying. He wants to know if you'll come home to take over the family interests."

Short and to the point, Bernson thought.

Barnes frowned. His long ginger hair, which had moved continually in the breeze and more so while he walked, seemed to go still momentarily and settle closer to his head.

He knitted his fingers together and looked calmly at Jakes. "Mr. Jakes, I appreciate your efforts to find me. I'm genuinely saddened to hear this news about Father.

"But we Barnes are strong folk. Father instilled in me the means to determine my way, and tempered the iron to see it through.

"I've chosen this relatively uncharted path, here with the Kkorchbe, and I intend to stay, despite Father's wishes. He made me the Barnes I am. And while he may not understand my decision, he'll certainly understand why I've made it and will stand by it."

Jakes looked a little disappointed, but the smile that appeared on his face almost seemed wistful to Bernson. "I see," the American said. "I'm dependent on my companions for travel back to the coast, so I'll be here until Mr. Bernson determines it's time to leave. Until then, perhaps you will consider the offer and maybe change your mind. Your decision at the time we leave I must consider final.

"But please keep in mind that once you turn down the offer, your access to the family funds will be cut off. Permanently."

Barnes noted. "So noted, Mr. Jakes."

Bernson lifted one eyebrow and cut a glance at Ki-Gor. Jakes had just demonstrated more composure than anyone had witnessed since he'd set foot on the continent. Rather than allaying the guide's suspicions, Jakes' interchange with Barnes had only made Bernson more alert to keeping an eye on his client.

Ki-Gor, for his part, stared at Jakes, but revealed no change of expression.

Barnes had moved his attention to Moore. "What brings you and your fascinating conveyance to our remote corner of the Congo?"

Moore beamed like a complimented school boy, and his red mustache rose with his smile. "I'm working with the Royal Geographic Society and the British Museum," he explained, "following some research on exotic flora and fauna, um, particularly rare, that are believed to inhabit your, eh, 'remote corner.'"

Barnes' face brightened. "Perhaps we can help you. The Kkorchbe are very familiar with all the local animals."

"Yes, hm." Moore now looked a bit embarrassed. "Perhaps we'll find a way for you to help us in our efforts. Thank you."

"The Kkorchbe tell me many legends about many creatures and people that live in the jungle," Barnes explained, "and while I discount many of them, perhaps there is a kernel of truth at the heart of some of these stories. Unlikely, I concede, but the stories have persisted."

Dr. Moore nodded. "These stories are reported by explorers and ethnographers. And so the Royal Society and the British Museum have sent my expedition."

The tone of Barnes' voice was flat. "There are many legends about the mysteries of Africa. I admit that some such stories attracted me here. But these tales of mysterious creatures, Dr. Moore, you may be as fortunate in locating a surviving dodo bird."

Moore shrugged. "I have found many unexpected delights in the Congo, my new friend, Mr. Ki-Gor, here, is one, so I shall have to follow the requirements of my mission as best I can: to find the beasts or to provide reasonable documentation to determine the fictional basis of these stories."

Barnes spread his hands and shrugged in return.

Moore sent word to the crew of the *Pegasus* that the party would stay in the Kkorchbe's kraal. NSomu and the other porters hired by Bernson refused to come to the kraal. Neither would they stay in the airship, its lighter-than-air qualities seemed utterly unnatural to them, and so they camped in the fields below the craft, making sure their camp lay nowhere that the *Pegasus*' shadow fell.

The airship stayed above like a silver, stationary cloud tethered to the ground.

The night passed quietly.

The next day, however, was completely different.

When Ki-Gor and his party had first boarded the *Pegasus*, Msoulewaki had been an enthusiastic guide for the newcomers, showing them the wonders of the flying machine like a proud owner, ending his tour with the large observation port. The view overlooking miles of treetops nearly took away Ki-Gor's breath.

But since arriving at the Kkorchbe's kraal, Msoulewaki was very subdued.

Early the second day in the pygmies' camp, Ki-Gor approached his new friend. They were not close to anyone and so enjoyed some privacy. "Is all well, Msoulewaki?"

"I am uneasy about . . . I am not sure. Since we came here, something seems . . . unright. Perhaps I have been chased away by so many new tribes I meet, perhaps I am just waiting for that to happen again."

Ki-Gor nodded, looked across the communal area at Jakes. The American stood alone, staring at their host, Barnes, who conversed with three of the Kkorchbe.

Ki-Gor said, "I understand your feeling. Something does not seem right." He smiled and clapped Msoulewaki on the shoulder. "But perhaps we are both wrong." They joined Bernson and the rest for the morning meal.

As they walked, Ki-Gor saw the three Kkorchbe nod to Barnes and leave the kraal at a trot. Their host joined the main body of tribesmen and their visitors, a fresh smile on his face.

Jakes watched Barnes talk to the pygmies, then saw him walk away and smile.

Go ahead. Smile. You might not live out the day, Jakes thought.

He had hated most of this job. Jakes admitted this tour into the jungle had kept him out of his depth most of the time. He had been ill-prepared for this journey. He was at home in the jungles of the metropolitan areas of the United States, Britain, Europe. Getting here through the terrors of the jungle had simply been one waking nightmare after another for Jakes.

But now he was here. He'd been able to talk to Barnes and apply his strengths. He would simply have to get Barnes to sign a document explaining that he waived his claim to the family fortune. He had such a document in the materials brought on the trip. Once signed, it could be manipulated by his employers so that they, and their American partner, Joe the Shark, ended up with control of the funds through one or another business front.

In Jakes' mind, Barnes was an absolute fool. Choosing to stay in this miserable green hell when he had the chance for a fortune to be dropped in his lap, so he could live in luxury anywhere in the civilized world, there was nothing but complete stupidity in such a move, Jakes thought.

But Jakes would have to make sure that Barnes didn't renege or decide unexpectedly to spoil the works. Perhaps Barnes would take that tour of the airship and accidentally fall to his death. Or perhaps he might take a walk into the jungle, an absolutely deadly place for a man to have an accident, both unsurprising and fatal.

Jakes nodded to himself. He just would have to keep his eyes open, watch for his opportunity. He would have to make sure those busybodies, Ki-Gor, Moore, and the others, weren't around at the time. Jakes had managed to make these sorts of accidents happen before, quite successfully, in fact. He had a bit of expertise in this area. He just had to stay sharp.

He swam out of the pool of his own thoughts and noticed Ki-Gor and Bernson looking his way. He acted as though he hadn't noticed, but turned to join the others for the morning meal.

That's when everyone in the kraal heard the gunfire.

It was distant, perhaps from the direction of the *Pegasus.*

The meal was forgotten. Everyone hurried toward the entrance of the kraal.

Where they were stopped by more gunfire.

A group of men stood inside the Kkorchbe's kraal, strangers blocking the way, firing into the air.

Then they lowered the barrels of their weapons and pointed them at the people who had rushed to the entrance.

"Good morning," said the man who stood in front of the rest of the intruders. He smiled, but there was no humor in his face. "It's the start of a wonderful day."

🦁 🦁 🦁

Martin Grainger addressed his captives carefully. He kept an eye open for any tricks from these pygmies and their guests. The foppish one who looked entirely out of place, Brendan Barnes, caught Grainger's notice. "You," he said. "Translate what I say to the rest of this crowd."

He was tired from his labors, but energized by the capture of this tribe. He knew he was close to his objective, the gold of Ophir, and surely someone here knew where to find the mine.

Everything was working out quite well.

Then they lowered the barrels of their weapons and pointed them at the people...

The squad had come out the tunnel under the wall of foliage and reconnoitered just before dark last night. After a few hours rest, Martin Grainger assigned his men to their tasks for taking control of the area.

The setup had worked well for Grainger's men. Before daylight, they had easily rounded up the carriers camped near the airship. When the *Pegasus'* crew lowered its platform at dawn, three men were to overpower the platform's operator and get aboard to take over the craft.

The gunfire Grainger had heard from that direction might mean the effort had gone awry; if so, he now had plenty of hostages for making the airship's captain and crew amenable to his demands. Meanwhile, some of Grainger's men were outside the kraal to locate and subdue any Kkorchbe sentries.

Grainger allowed himself a smile. "So, good morning. We'll start our new relationship by everyone here dropping your weapons in a pile at my feet."

The prisoners grumbled but complied. Moore blustered, "Relationship? What do you mean?"

Grainger replied, "Killing you would be simplest for me. But we'll need help at the mine, and here in this kraal I now have a ready-made crew."

"Mine?" Moore looked from Grainger to Barnes. "What are you talking about?"

"Don't be coy. We're here for the same reason, I'm sure. Solomon's gold mine, of course."

"Land of Goshen!" exclaimed Msoulewaki.

Jakes barked, "Gold? There's gold?!"

Grainger scowled. He directed one of his men to collect the discarded weapons.

Bernson scowled as well. His revolver was in the pile of surrendered weapons, but he wondered if he would get a chance to retrieve his rifle, which was back in one of the huts.

Then he noticed that Ki-Gor was missing.

Where had the blond giant gone?

When the first gunfire burst had sounded, Ki-Gor had bounded out of the kraal on the side farthest from its entrance. His mighty leap brought him into the undergrowth between the kraal and the clearing containing the Kkorchbe's three catapults.

He crept toward that clearing, a lithe jungle cat slinking through the foliage, hearing the sound of chopping ahead.

At the clearing's edge, he found the body of one of the pygmies he'd seen talking to Barnes earlier. One of Grainger's men was busy disabling the trebuchets with an axe. A second stood guard, scanning the surroundings.

Ki-Gor slipped away. He rounded the greater area within which the kraal was located. He encountered two more Kkorchbe men, sentries who hadn't yet been subdued by Grainger's squad, and gestured for them to follow him quietly and keep a lookout for Grainger's men who might be scouring for anyone not herded within the kraal.

Billy McShane had been continually angry during this expedition, but he was actually pleased to be sent by Grainger to search out any pygmies who might be at large: they would offer some good target practice. He grinned at the thought.

Billy stopped. He couldn't believe his eyes. He'd stepped into a clearing, neatly trimmed and shaped very obviously like a baseball diamond and outfield.

Next he heard something, a hiss. In the half-second between turning and suddenly seeing stars, he saw, of all things, something that looked like a baseball. Spinning, hissing through the air, hurtling toward his face.

Billy saw stars.

Then all went black.

Ki-Gor bound the unconscious Billy with stout vines. He tested their tightness with satisfaction while one of the accompanying pygmies ground the end of the thug's weapon into the soil, packing the barrel end with dirt. Then the blond giant signaled, and the three trotted away with no more noise than a breeze through the leaves.

Grainger's man, who minutes before had been chopping at the Kkorchbe's trebuchet, now lay unconscious and tied, a purpling goose egg rising on his skull. Beside him lay his companion, also unconscious, with two black eyes from Ki-Gor's fists.

The two pygmies were busy repairing the least-damaged catapult. Ki-Gor provided the needed brute strength where directed. While they worked, Ki-Gor's gaze darted about frequently, and he tested the air with his jungle-honed sense of smell to check for approaching enemies.

Grainger was growing irritated. The men he'd sent out to secure the area hadn't yet returned.

He shrugged. Billy was brutal, and the others were quite competent. They could handle anything that came their ways. Nothing for Grainger to worry about.

He gestured with his gun. "Everyone back to the center of the kraal," he ordered. He wanted this crowd of prisoners tied down, then he and his men could eat and consider their next moves for securing the gold.

Then Grainger heard something from beyond the opposite side of the kraal. He looked up.

"Move!" he shouted.

A roaring fireball came streaking toward his position. Everyone scattered as the blazing missile crashed to the ground and exploded into a wider burst of flame.

"Come on!" Barnes shouted, and the prisoners surged out of the kraal, knocking over the confused gunmen, leaping over the burning debris as Grainger yelled to get his men back in order.

The Kkorchbe streamed various directions. Msoulewaki ran, found himself behind Jakes and Barnes, who called out, "The Kkorchbe have cached weapons. We'll soon rout these ruffians."

A stream of bullets tore the ground near the running trio, and Barnes shifted direction. Msoulewaki cast a look back: Grainger and four others chased, firing.

Msoulewaki noted that Barnes was surprisingly spry as he zagged and zigged. Jakes, too.

The American eccentric led them past massive tree boles and through a sort of rough gateway, an upthrust of lichen-covered boulders. The opening quickly funneled down to a narrow defile that twisted side to side. Barnes hurried on.

Jakes gasped, "We'll be trapped in here!"

"Come on," Barnes urged. The sounds of their pursuers entering the gateway, their weapons occasionally scraping the stone walls, reached the hunted men.

The corridor slanted downward, continuing to twist through the rocks. The three reached a fork. Barnes paused, shouted, "To the left!" and darted that way.

Jakes growled, "Idiot! They heard you!"

Barnes continued trotting along the crack in the stone, sometimes turning sideways to fit, not pausing a moment.

The trio heard one of the pursuers say, "This way!" when the gunmen reached the fork, and the subsequent sounds of pursuit made clear that Barnes and his companions were not alone in their fork of the trail.

Msoulewaki could smell the sweat coming off Jakes. He could hear the man grunt with each step, and his breath was growing more labored.

Barnes stopped. Before them was a large break in the wall on the left. Sunlight streamed into the narrow cavity through the hole. Thirty feet away was the other edge of the opening, and the defile through the stone continued.

Their leader raised a finger to his lips. He turned away, tiptoed to the edge of the opening.

Jakes' features changed. This was his chance. He bent, pulled an object from his boot, touched a stud on its side, and a shiny blade snapped into place.

Paralysis gripped Msoulewaki. His mouth opened, but no sound emerged as Jakes drove forward, knife raised.

Barnes, ignorant of the immediate danger, dashed across the opening to the enclosed trail on its other side.

Jakes nearly stumbled as his swing missed Barnes. But he didn't continue pursing his target. Instead, standing in the opening, exposed to the sun, he turned and gaped at something Msoulewaki couldn't see beyond the walls of the defile.

There was a rush of wind and a SNAP!

Jakes was gone.

The open knife lay shining in the sunlight on the ground between Msoulewaki and Barnes.

Msoulewaki screamed, "The serpent! The serpent! Satan's come to take us to Hell!"

Barnes was calling for Msoulewaki to join him, but Msoulewaki couldn't hear the American. Nor could he hear the swiftly approaching gunmen.

He was rooted to the spot, staring at the place from which Jakes had disappeared, as if hypnotized by the gleaming knife.

"Satan!" Msoulewaki cried out again.

"It's not Satan!" Barnes yelled. "Get over here! Quick!"

Too late, Msoulewaki became aware the gunmen were right behind him. A gun barrel pressed against his ribs. "Hold on, boys," said a gruff voice.

Before another move could be made, the four gunmen slammed forward, smashing into Msoulewaki, who stumbled along the trail, then screamed and fell off the path and through the opening.

Barnes swore, then clambered swiftly down the boulders that marked the slope from the opening in the defile to the level ground twenty feet below.

Ki-Gor and his pygmy companions had gotten the trebuchet operational and sent the burning missile into the kraal. In the resulting confusion, the two pygmies had laid low any enemies they crossed by beaning them with their handmade baseballs. Soon they were joined by the other Kkorchbe, who had retrieved their cached weapons.

Ki-Gor had spotted Barnes, Jakes and Msoulewaki being chased. He took off after them at a run.

The jungle giant had crashed into Grainger's gunmen from behind in the tight confines of the defile. Now he swung his fists like pounding sledges, thrashing the four men in the opening in the stone corridor.

"Ki-Gor!" Barnes called out just as one of the four grabbed a dropped gun and began firing.

The blond giant dodged, leaped into space. He landed atop a boulder and leaped again, just as gunfire splintered the surface of his perch.

In this way he reached Barnes, hunkered down in the shade of large tree standing near a massive rock. At his knees lay Msoulewaki, who clutched one leg and held back groans behind tight lips.

Ki-Gor examined Msoulewaki's leg. "Broken," Barnes said.

Ki-Gor nodded. He heard the gunmen scrabbling down the rocky face of the slope. He scanned the surroundings. Jungle growth was thick at their backs, and rock walls blocked any passage before them.

"The jungle, then," Ki-Gor said, and he lifted Msoulewaki gently, with little apparent strain.

Msoulewaki's face looked desperate. "Satan!" he cried.

A puzzled look crossed Ki-Gor's face. "It's not Satan, I said," Barnes said.

Ki-Gor cast a glance at their pursuers getting nearer. "Let's go," he said, and carried Msoulewaki into the tangled green, Barnes close behind.

Martin Grainger paused at the bottom of the rocky slope. His quarry had disappeared. "Flanking maneuver," he directed. The four men separated and entered the jungle. Grainger took the left course.

Ki-Gor paused in his rush through the jungle growth. Barnes quickly caught up. He leaned against a tree to catch his breath, he had never seen anyone move so fast as the jungle man.

Ki-Gor lowered Msoulewaki so he rested with his back against a tree. Then he stood very still. His keen hearing picked up the sounds of the four gunmen starting to move into the thick jungle, slowly, cautiously. But there was something else as well. Something he couldn't identify.

"Wait here," he said to Barnes, then he leaped into the limbs above their heads and disappeared into the leafy green.

Barnes was clearly startled by Ki-Gor's disappearance. Msoulewaki grimaced against the pain, but still managed to say, "That's how the Tree Man works. He's here, then he's not."

Up in the middle terrace formed by the arboreal giants, Ki-Gor whipped through the air and from branch to branch until he found a spot where the breeze brought him a sure scent. He stopped, perched high above the ground. He sniffed the air. Again.

He heard something moving through the jungle. Something large. At this height in the trees he could detect a slight vibration of its footsteps. He could hear its hide scrape against the boles of trees, the crackle of breaking shrubs. Otherwise, it moved with a terrible silence.

And he could detect its scent. But he could not identify the source. Ki-Gor thought at first his nose still was affected by the bay rum Jakes had worn, but he decided this was a scent he had never encountered before.

The jungle man returned to his companions. "There's something moving around out there. Something besides those men with guns," he said.

"It's the serpent," Msoulewaki said. "It's Satan."

Barnes shook his head. Before he could say a word, Ki-Gor disappeared again into the leafy branches above their heads.

Grainger's man who patrolled on the right flank moved steadily, listening intently for any sounds that might reveal his quarry. Trees and vines and shadows crisscrossed in every direction, tricking the eyes. He paused. Was that a whispering voice?

"Hey."

He looked up. The jungle man was swinging down from the crown of a tree. Grainger's man had only a split-second view of Ki-Gor before his military training kicked in, and although he quickly raised his gun, his finger already tightening on the trigger, he still didn't have time to aim before Ki-Gor slammed into his chest. He scrambled, breathless but full of fight, and again raised his weapon, but only saw the blond giant raise his knife and swing before all went dark.

The second gunman advanced warily. If the flankers started a crossfire, he didn't want to end up in the middle of it, so he didn't want to advance as quickly as they moved through their sections of forest.

The jungle growth was thick here. He kept alert. Eyes moving steadily from side to side, changing the position of his head slightly to get a different perspective on the slanting and crossing shadows and branches and leaves, he wanted to find his quarry before they spotted him.

Even, steady steps. Careful of too much noise.

He stopped to listen. What was that?

He heard a whisper in the trees.

His gaze traveled up the bole of an ancient, vine-twisted tree.

"Hey."

Grainger stayed at the edge of the jungle, keeping an eye on the bouldered slope that led to the precipitous stone walls in case his quarry attempted to return to the opening and escape back to the defile that brought them here.

He moved slowly. He was a man of action, but he was also a cautious man. His many missions conducted on behalf of Caspar Kovacevich's desires for obtaining more esoteric *objets d'art* and treasures from distant lands had trained him to be careful in all things when dealing with dangerous adversaries. And Grainger had seen that jungle man at work in the green barrier outside the pygmy territory, he wasn't going to risk not finding Kovacevich's gold by underestimating that jungle savage.

The fighting skills Grainger had honed through multiple perilous missions were primed to kick into gear at the slightest twitch of something moving in the jungle that might be the men he was tracking. The men he had sent in a spread-out formation had yet to encounter the men they pursued, or he would have heard something from them by now.

This near-naked jungle man was clearly a formidable enemy. He might make a good slave to work in the mine, when Grainger found it, the blond giant could probably out-work two or three other men. But Grainger sensed the jungle man would be too dangerous to keep around. As soon as he was located, Grainger planned to cut him down immediately.

Grainger continued his slow advance. He carefully scanned the treetops, the boles, the ground.

There.

Something caught his eye. He walked over, bent down, picked it up.

Grainger had hardly stood upright again when he heard a furious rushing through the trees. He looked up.

He saw a great gaping maw of massive teeth.

A grinding SNAP followed.

"Satan!" hissed Msoulewaki.

He was hunkered behind a massive tree trunk with Barnes and Ki-Gor.

"Hush! Not Satan," Barnes whispered. "It's a bloody dinosaur."

The giant beast reared upward, its maw wide, dripping gore. The massive head turned slowly.

"Mokele-mbembe," Ki-Gor breathed. "I've heard of this giant thunder lizard. But even I thought that here was one tale that was just that, a legend."

"Another of the Congo's mysteries," Barnes said. "One that not even my curiosity has driven me to learn more about. They live cutoff in this great valley, contained by these high walls, locally, at least. On beyond," he swung his arm outward from the way they had come, "I have no idea."

The beast continued to stand and turn its head this way and that, slowly, in a ponderous manner that belied how quickly it had moved when Ki-Gor and his companions saw it attack Grainger. It raised its snout, as it sniffing the air.

"I don't like the looks of this," Ki-Gor whispered.

"From skeletons I saw in museums, I'd say it's related to a tyrannosaurus Rex," Barnes said. "But it looks different somehow—or perhaps I just don't recognize it from the artist renderings I saw in books."

Ki-Gor shushed the American.

The monster from another time again turned its head, then swung it toward the three men's hiding place. It began to advance, in a hurry.

"Sit still," Ki-Gor said, then he shot into the branches with a flicker of movement.

The jungle man dropped back into sight from the trees to the ground right in the path the T Rex was taking toward its prey. The monster slowed just a moment, as though startled by Ki-Gor's sudden appearance. Then the blond giant dashed away to the left, shouting insults he'd learned from the monkeys near his home.

With a rush, the beast swerved after the blond giant. Now that it had speed, its steps thundered on the ground and Ki-Gor could feel the earth shaking beneath his feet. The dinosaur slammed past trees, wrenching the massive boles from the earth, roots and all. Great, rending cracks accompanied its rush as it shattered branches and trees in its path.

Ki-Gor's mighty legs launched him into the trees again. The beast slowed, its head darted side to side. Then the blond giant dropped from the canopy and landed atop the creature's back.

He had his knife in his hand, and he drove its razor-edged blade through the beast's thick hide to help him maintain his position on the back of the dinosaur. Then the monster swung about, its massive tail cutting a deadly arc through the air, smashing to splinters any trees in its way. If Barnes had witnessed the scene, he would have compared it to a cowboy riding a bucking bronco, something he had seen in a moving picture at a theatre in Boston.

Ki-Gor clung tightly, then began making his way up the creature's neck, stretching his arm and driving his knife into the dinosaur's flesh to serve as a series of handholds toward the giant head.

The monster continued to thrash about, attempting to fling whatever annoyance clung to its back. Because of its size, the knife thrusts were little more than annoyances, but those annoyance's continuing was enraging the beast.

Ki-Gor had reached the bony head of the dinosaur. His legs and arms were wrapped about the muscular neck. He lifted one arm, holding tight his knife. He planned to blind the monster in a first step in his effort to kill it.

Then the great head jerked around, snapped about, and Ki-Gor was flung from his hold. He flailed through the air and thudded against a tree. He slid to the ground, dazed.

Still the monster did not roar or utter any other sound. It spotted Ki-Gor, this irritant that had been upon its back, and its mighty legs drove it forward to snap up the blond giant in its massive jaws, just as it had gobbled up Jakes and Grainger with a sudden snap!

Ki-Gor saw stars, but the sudden life-or-death realm of the jungle had trained his skills so that he leapt away from the rushing jaws just as they cracked together. He spun across the ground, jumped and surged up the flank of the beast to reach the ridge of its backbone. From there he leaped into the branches of the trees.

The thunder lizard's tail rushed through the air and smashed against the tree in which Ki-Gor perched. The blond giant tumbled from one branch to another, then leaped again to another tree, then another, rushing through the tangle of branches just as he had when GTongo and his sons had been firing arrows at him in their test of skill.

One tree, then another cracked and splintered as the beast swept its tail about, seeking to dislodge the jumping pest from its leafy hiding spots.

Finally the monster was rewarded when it smashed a tree and Ki-Gor flew from the canopy and thudded to the ground. He rolled and came to his feet. He snarled. His knife was raised, ready for battle to the death.

Then a low sound, *Harrrrrooooooooooo*, like the bellow of a sort of horn sounded from a great distance. The beast's scaled head turned to listen, then the monster galloped away through the jungle.

Ki-Gor, stunned, watched the monster crash into the jungle and disappear.

"Land of Goshen, was that a horn, calling it?" Msoulewaki gasped. His face was bathed in sweat. "Is it trained?"

Ki-Gor, bruised and scratched, had returned to Barnes and Msoulewaki and told them what had happened.

"Again, a mystery," Barnes admitted. "They utter no roars or noises. They go when called. In the Congo, mysteries lie within mysteries."

Ki-Gor nodded, then picked up Msoulewaki. "Let's get you back."

The three returned to the opening in the wall and the slanting trail. They passed the place Grainger had met his end, seeming not to notice a hand lying on the ground, clutching a stone.

A stone the size of a baseball.

A stone of solid gold.

The trio returned to the defile by moving from boulder to boulder, keeping watch for more giant reptiles. At the opening, Ki-Gor cast a last look at the hidden valley, wondering at the mysteries and adventure it might hide.

If that thunder lizard had a master, the beast's knife wounds might mean whoever controlled the creature would come investigating.

At the kraal, the pygmies tended the wounded and guarded their bound attackers, those who survived. Moore and Bernson warmly greeted Barnes, Ki-Gor and Msoulewaki, and Dr. Moore examined the latter's leg.

Bernson showed his terrible teeth in a wide grin as he clapped Ki-Gor's shoulder. "I wondered where you'd got to," the small guide said.

"The *Pegasus*?" Ki-Gor asked.

"The airship's fine," Moore said. "This lot underestimated her crew. Crack military unit manning the vessel. Some of my personal staff from Department Q at MI6. Some of the men will be here soon with the ship's doctor."

He looked around. "Where's the crowd that was after you? One of them, rogue named Grainger, was the leader."

"Dead," Ki-Gor announced.

"And Jakes?"

"Dead, too."

Moore noted the giant's expression and asked no more questions.

While returning through the defile, Ki-Gor and Msoulewaki had agreed to Barnes' request not to mention the hidden valley. If more men knew its secrets, more invaders were sure to come. For scientific purposes, or other reasons more base.

"The gold?" Ki-Gor had asked Barnes on the trip back to the kraal.

"Who knows if Grainger's claim was true or just the result of some man's greed dream?" Barnes shrugged. "The Kkorchbe have never mentioned to me if they've explored the valley or whether they found gold. They seem uninterested, for some reason."

Later, Moore revealed how his connection to Department Q had launched his journey. "We learned Jakes had been sent here by an unscrupulous band with connections to the American underworld. Other unsavory elements on the Continent, as well. We've been studying them for some time. But Jakes had a jump on us, apparently he'd left for the interior with Bernson before I reached the coast.

"But he was right about your father, Barnes. I can offer you conveyance back to civilization if you wish to claim your inheritance."

"My earlier response stands, Doctor." Barnes smiled over a steaming cup of local tea.

Moore nodded his large, red-haired head. "We learned from a William McShane, particularly vile mouth on that one, of Grainger's recent adventures. Explains a bit about an Arabic uprising to the north. The *Pegasus* will be leaving in forty-eight hours to report back, Department Q will wrap up the miscreants behind these misadventures, though the Royal Society will be further disappointed my commandeering their craft will have cut short their expedition's goals. But I can take anyone with us who wants to go."

That included Ki-Gor, GTongo, NTongo, NGonto, and Bernson. Even NSomu and the carriers Bernson had hired for Jakes were willing to board the airship again, anything to leave behind this isolated Devil's Nest.

"And you, Msoulewaki?" Dr. Moore asked.

Msoulewaki sat with his bound leg stretched before him. "I have Mr. Barnes and the Kkorchbe's permission to stay. I have been like Jonah, the Word of God kept directing me this way, but I continued trying to go my own way elsewhere. But finally I am somewhere I won't be chased away."

Moore smiled. "As you wish."

Ki-Gor rubbed one of his aching shoulders and asked, "What was the *Pegasus*' mission you interrupted?"

Moore barked a little laugh. "Some Society patron funded an expedition to locate, of all things—a dinosaur. You know, one of those giant, prehistoric lizards. Too close a follower of that old crackpot Challenger, I suppose." Moore shook his head. "This is the Congo, not some cloud-shrouded neverland like Maple White Land."

Barnes guffawed. "Indeed, sir. Indeed." His ginger hair flew about his head and his eyes twinkled as he looked at Ki-Gor.

Paris

Caspar Kovacevich sat in an uncomfortable wooden chair before a large mahogany desk, the chair of which was empty. He had been here, alone, for more than an hour.

An officer from the Surete had arrived at his home, named Gaboriau, something like that—and escorted him to the police headquarters and this room. Kovacevich had been in this situation, in rooms like this one, many times before. Sometimes the wait was only a few minutes, the longest had lasted three hours. In each case, the solitude ended with the arrival of some official, a police inspector, a representative of the port authority, an officer of the court, whose interrogation revealed someone's interest in his comings and goings, his business dealings. These matters typically were cleared up by his answers, responses from an acquaintance to whom a messenger was dispatched, or the words from some government bureaucrat whose familiarity Kovacevich had been careful to cultivate in the past. In any event, Caspar always was released and allowed to return home before the end of the day.

Kovacevich expected similar treatment today. Who knew whose conscience had been tweaked, what papers had caught the eye of some clerk, that led to his being summoned here? Caspar was very busy, and any number of his dealings may have resulted in this call. Gregor would be fine, for the housekeeper would see to the boy after school hours. Kovacevich remained calm, for such occurrences were part of his business. He knew how this world worked. That knowledge and his mastery of it allowed him to accumulate the treasures he loved.

A second hour had already passed when the door opened and a smartly dressed man with pince nez entered and stood behind the desk facing Caspar. The man held a single sheet of paper, which he reviewed silently before looking up at the seated figure. "Monsieur, I am François Schuiten," he introduced himself, then crisply inclined his head for a moment as a sort of bow to Kovacevich, as though he would allow only this slight bit of formal courtesy to slow his business.

"I represent the Belgian embassy. I am here regarding your involvement in an unfriendly incursion into territories belonging to my country, namely The Congo."

A twinge of anxiety curled in Caspar's gut. "Pardon me?"

"Also of interest is your relationship with an armed force that sought control of a portion of that territory, including that of a British citizen named Martin Grainger, now deceased."

The shield of calm that Caspar had carried now melted. "Monsieur?"

"These are serious matters," Schuiten continued. "And I respectfully recommend you consider them carefully. How you deal with me may help you in dealing with, or not having to deal with, other gentlemen from other interested governments."

"Other governments?" Caspar felt the warm presence of sweat on his scalp.

Schuiten glanced at the sheet of paper. "Something about the theft from an American manufacturer of prototype arms and ammunition intended for the Army of the United States of America." He didn't glance up before adding, "And a representative of the British government has questions about your knowledge of efforts to incite revolution in the Sudan."

As Caspar felt his palms suddenly go clammy, he knew this interrogation would not go so smoothly as all the rest.

Boston

John Edward Felton, a stout and healthy young man who had felt more at ease in recent weeks than he had in months, those months having been marked by an ever-growing anxiety associated with Joe the Shark and a large sum of money due him, stood with his hand on a doorknob, arrested in his tracks by the sight of George Duke Buckingham's desk: unoccupied.

Felton had been summoned to Buckingham's office. Where was Buckingham? The old man, in Felton's memory, never had left his desk.

"Close the door, Mr. Felton."

Felton received a shock when he heard Buckingham speak from across the room. The gaunt old man in his out-of-style suit stood before a tall window. Another surprise: the shutters were open, and light streamed into the room in a steep slant that appeared almost solid, as if Buckingham were immobilized within a bar of honey-colored amber.

But the old man wasn't immobile. His domed head turned so that his bulging eyes peered over the sharp point of his shoulder at Felton, still standing before the door, now closed, not at all at ease. "Sit down, Mr. Felton."

Buckingham turned, a slow movement that seemed to Felton as though the body, tethered to the old man's large head by his thin neck, simply followed the orb above the shirt collar, and approached the clerk, keeping the desk between the two men. Buckingham's hands were clasped behind his back.

"Do you follow the sport of baseball, Mr. Felton?"

The young man couldn't take his gaze from Buckingham's bulging eyes. He wondered if the old man were succumbing to some illness. Never had Felton heard Buckingham utter a syllable about any matter that didn't regard the legal profession and the firm's business. "Um, I've attended a few games, yes sir." He'd lost money on them, too.

"I fear Heinie Wagner's boys are going to let us down hard this year," Buckingham said. The somber expression didn't move from his face. "Bill McKechnie may have a better team. I suspect Philadelphia, however, will be the team to beat. But one's devotion to the venerable Red Sox should remain unshaken. One must be loyal."

Felton simply nodded. He expected any moment now to see the old man to collapse in a heap on the floor, panting for breath.

Instead, Buckingham strode back to the sunlit window, his steps quite steady. "Baseball is a particular sport that creates loyalty in hearts and minds that might otherwise have no loyalty to anyone or anything other than their own existence. I have seen fiercely independent men who have leaned on the support of no other person, who have acquired vast sums of money through their own energies and minds and are beholden to no one, yet I have seen them weep at the outcome of a Sunday afternoon double header." The old man closed his eyes, tilted back his head, and seemed to bask in the light coming through the panes. "Perhaps this loyalty starts as a childhood enthusiasm for a game, and this love of play grows into love of a team and the magic of potential performance."

His head turned suddenly toward Felton, who flinched. "I played baseball as a youngster. As a young man. Not for money, Mr. Felton, no, simply for the joy of the game. Hurling a ball from the outfield to catch a runner at home plate, a sort of race, if you will. Standing in at shortstop for an absent teammate. Jousting with the pitcher, to get on base despite his spitball tricks. Ah."

Buckingham's large eyes stared at the clerk without blinking. "No matter the number of fielding errors, the number of strikeouts, it is the potential, what a fan knows a team's possibilities may be, regardless of the scoreboard's illustrating what they are, that carries the loyal follower through the season from game to game. And despite disappointments, the fan is loyal, because one knows that the team and the game depend on rules. The rules make the game work, make the team focus on turning potentialities into reality so that it deserves that loyalty. One might say the team makes the loyalty its fans direct its way by recognizing the rules, playing within them, making them work."

A pause, then: "Mr. Felton, you have broken the rules."

If the clerk had been confused since entering the room, now a cold flash of panic stabbed his guts. "S-sir?"

"Our clients are loyal to our firm because we know the rules of our profession. They rely upon us to follow those rules and to work in their interest. We do so, and therefore deserve their loyalty. But when the rules are broken…"

Felton had difficulty breathing.

"When a clerk defies the rules of our profession, when he disregards the loyalty of our clients to further his own interests…"

Felton stifled a dry, hacking sob.

"When he consorts with criminals to seek the benefit of others at the expense of our clients, perhaps at the cost of a life…"

In the blink of an eye, Buckingham, belying his age and seeming infirmities, whipped about and threw a baseball. It rocketed across the room with a short rush of sound and smacked Felton in the chest.

The young man rocked back in his chair and smashed to the floor. After the flashing of stars subsided from his sight and he caught his breath, he saw Buckingham bending over him, roaring with the vigor of a man half a century younger:

"Mr. Felton, I own baseballs signed by Ty Cobb, Cy Young, and Walter Johnson. As you begin to learn what loyalty really means, you may start your own collection with this one." Buckingham thrust a baseball before Felton's eyes. It once had belonged to a man named Billy McShane. Signed in large letters across the horsehide were the words *I'm sure you'll do fine without me* and the name *Brendan Barnes*.

The Congo

Thwack!

Helene's anger, fed by her worry over Ki-Gor's extended absence, despite a message from Tembu George, had abated finally. When her husband and his companions had returned, with Ki-Gor bearing a gift from the Kkorchbe, a cushion covered in a flawless white hide, to Tchamba's village, Tchamba had been delighted when Ki-Gor had offered him and his family, including the baby, a ride in that miraculous wonder, an airship.

Helene suspected much of this show was merely Ki-Gor's effort to avoid a tongue lashing from his wife.

But Helene's buoyant, boyish husband, who could play games with the exuberance of a child with his friends, would defend from any threat those he loved like an enraged lion, or would battle an enemy to the death with the bloodthirstiness of the fiercest warrior, hugged and kissed her with the fervor of a man who had greatly missed his loved one, and he could not wait to recount his latest adventures. Ki-Gor was utterly transparent. There was no subterfuge about him. His love and loyalty were threaded throughout every fibre of his mightily muscled frame.

And now Helene watched him at play again. In a game he'd brought back from some crackpot American, willingly lost in the Congo, a game she thought she'd never see again.

Tembu George stood at the home-made home plate, swinging a smoothly hewn bat. N'Geeso, pygmy king of a village of mighty warriors, some of whom roved the outfield, stood atop the pitcher's mound.

Tembu George called out, "Helene, can you smell me?"

"Yes, I do, Tembu George." Ki-Gor had presented his friends bottles of bay rum he'd confiscated from the baggage of the villains he'd defeated during his journey. The giant warrior seemed to enjoy bathing his body in the fragrance.

"Do I smell manly?" He grinned with a fierce joy.

"I'm sure you do," Helene smiled and tried not to giggle.

"Every woman of my tribe will crave my attention," the batter announced.

"Not if they see you in action on this field of battle," N'Geeso cried.

"Play ball!" Ki-Gor shouted from second base.

"Throw the ball!" Tembu George commanded.

N'Geeso complied. The pill smacked Tembu George right in the solar plexus, and the giant warrior sat down with a thud. His eyes were wide as he gasped for breath. N'Geeso and his outfielders cackled.

Tembu George swayed to his feet, then raised the bat and rushed the mound. N'Geeso scrambled to the outfield, then back around the infield, the giant warrior in pursuit.

"Home run!" shouted Ki-Gor, and the outfield pygmies hurrahed.

Helene sighed. Her lord of the jungle was, thankfully, back home.

THE END

Notes for "The Devil's Nest"

Parts of this story are rather fanciful. That's why we enjoy jungle adventure stories, right? On the other hand, some elements are quite real.

The eccentric American expatriate, Brendan Barnes, was a real person.

Sort of.

Patrick Tracy Lowell Putnam (1904-1953) was a member of a rich and famous family from Lowell, Massachusetts. The situation I describe for Brendan Barnes is quite different than for Putnam, but the latter spent twenty-five years living with the Bambuti pygmies of the Ituri Forest in what is now Zaire. Putnam was at least as eccentric as the fictional Barnes. Perhaps more so. His story is well told by Joan Mark in her book about Putnam, *The King of the World in the Land of the Pygmies* (Lincoln, Nebraska: University of Nebraska Press, 1995).

Meanwhile, the barrier of foliage that Ki-Gor and his companions encounter and try to hack their way through is very real. Outdoor writer David Quammen wrote a three-part article for *National Geographic* magazine about biologist J. Michael Fay's 1,200-mile hike through the Congo ("Megatransect," in the October 2000, March 2001, and August 2001 issues). In part 2, "Green Abyss," Quammen describes the barrier that the biologist encountered:

"... gradually they found themselves submerged in a swale of vegetation unlike anything Fay had ever seen."

Trained as a botanist long before he did his doctoral dissertation on gorillas, Fay describes it as "a solid sea of Marantaceae"—the family Marantaceae constituting a group of herbaceous tropical plants that includes gangly species such as Haumania liebrechtsiana, which can grow into stultifying thickets, denser than sugar cane, denser than grass, dense as the fur on a duck dog. The Marantaceae brake that Fay and his team had now entered, just east of the Sangha, stretched westward for God-knew-how-far. Fay himself, with a GPS unit and a half-decent map but no godlike perspective, knew not.

All he could do was point Mambeleme into the stuff, like a human Weedwacker, and fall in behind.

Sometimes they moved only 60 steps an hour. During one ten-hour day they made less than a mile.

You can find links to the three parts of the article at this URL: http://ngm.nationalgeographic.com/ngm/0010/feature1/index.html

Just as Pliny the Elder said, there's always something new out of old Africa.

DUANE SPURLOCK - is a writer, editor, and illustrator residing in Kentucky, where he and his wife and their children garden, draw, and tell stories to one another. Occasionally they whistle. He maintains a blog, The Spur & Lock Mercantile:

(http://spurandlock.blogspot.com/)

KI-GOR
&
THE SECRET OF THE
VIKINGS

By W. Peter Miller

T here was never silence in the jungle. That was something Ki-Gor, the Jungle Lord knew. He had traveled far up the Congo River with his bride, Helene, when he noticed. He stopped paddling, and his red-headed wife stopped too.

She looked at him expectantly and asked, "What is it, Ki-Gor?"

"The sound," he said.

The former New York society girl turned her head and listened. "I don't hear anything."

The Lord of the Jungle was visibly worried. "That's just it. No birds. No chatter of monkeys. There is no sound at all."

In the distance upriver, he could see a majestic waterfall streaming water out of a deep narrow canyon. It must have taken millennia to carve that two hundred foot high, narrow gash in the rock. There was a series of plateaus rising up in elevation beyond the waterfall.

Ki-Gor had never journeyed to those high plateaus. The Masai and the Mbuti told legends about them and wouldn't travel there. After hearing the stories, Ki-Gor was curious about the knife cat, the thunder horse, and other mythological beasts the stories told of. He wanted to see if those legends were true, especially the ones about the white Africans.

Helene's radiant red hair swirled in the wind. A sudden chill came over her. Up on the highest elevations, a huge, black, rolling storm cloud spilled down the mountain.

Lightning sparked and flashed and they saw torrents of rain hammering the high plains. The storm was moving toward them fast. Thunder shook the land.

Ki-Gor looked at Helene and commanded, "Turn." His arms pushed his paddle deep into the water and turned the canoe. Their expedition up river was at an end. Helene put her shoulder into it and they headed downstream. They knew they had to get away fast; away from the storm and the floods that were surely headed their way.

It wasn't long before the water began to rise. A noticeable swell passed under the canoe. Helene gripped the sides but relaxed as the high water passed under them. She went back to paddling.

A few minutes later, Ki-Gor felt a powerful rush of rainwater pass under them. It propelled the canoe forward down the river. He looked back and saw black clouds dumping sheets of rain down on the mountain. He had not seen a storm like this in many years. He dug his paddle deep into the water and hoped they would get far enough down river before the flood came.

Helene turned back to him and she saw the full force of the storm. Her face went white and her lip trembled in fear.

"Row!" Ki-Gor said, urging her on. She dug into the water. Ki-Gor did, too. He pushed the paddle so hard he feared it would break, but it held.

The water crested the banks and Ki-Gor kept the canoe in the center of the widening river. Tree roots were soon submerged and the waters rose ever higher. They paddled hard for miles, the river's might pushing them along as it rose.

Ki-Gor estimated that the river had risen ten feet when two frightened elephants crashed out of the jungle. A huge bull with eight-foot tusks knocked trees out of his way. A cow followed in his wake. Their frightful rush drove them into the river before they could turn.

Ki-Gor dug his paddle in the water, pushed against the flood, and tried to avoid the panicked pachyderms. The canoe steered slowly; fought the current. The Jungle Lord leveraged harder. He had almost steered past the beasts when his paddle snapped!

The raging current pushed the canoe straight for the enormous bull elephant's head. Helene was eye to eye with it. She screamed and jumped back just as the elephant flipped the canoe with its tusks. The wooden canoe splintered into the air and Ki-Gor and Helene flew. They crashed into the churning water.

Helene was tossed and spun as she fought to reach the surface. Ki-Gor didn't fight and let the water carry him. He got his bearings and saw Helene up river and above him. Her form was silhouetted against the lighter sky. She swam frantically. The female elephant was on a collision course with her.

Ki-Gor swam hard, but feared he would be too late. The elephant reached her and scooped the redhead up with her trunk. Ki-Gor broke the surface and saw the elephant set Helene gently on its neck. The female pachyderm looked at Ki-Gor and he gratefully extended his arm to her. She wrapped her trunk around it and hoisted him up.

The Jungle Lord dropped down on the elephant's neck in front of his wife. Helene wrapped her arms around him and buried her face in his shoulder.

The storm arrived over them. Lightning crashed and thunder shook the world. The rain beat them down like a club.

Ki-Gor looked back at the high canyon and saw the river spray out in a one hundred-foot high tower of water. Then the rock gave way, increasing the width of the opening ten-fold. Water and mountain gushed out at a ferocious rate and the jungle man knew they had to get to high ground fast.

He rubbed the elephant behind the ears and spoke to her in the way he had learned when he befriended Marmo. He hoped she would listen. The female elephant swam toward the shore.

As they neared it, Ki-Gor turned and kissed Helene. He said, "I'll be right back."

Ki-Gor stood, climbed over the swimming pachyderm's head, and slid down her trunk. He turned and looked into the beast's eyes. The elephant wrapped him in her trunk so that he wouldn't fall. Ki-Gor was exhausted and soaked through to the marrow, but he gestured vigorously at a spot on the shore where a break in the trees led upward.

When they reached the shore, the elephant hesitated. She looked nervously at the muddy bank. Ki-Gor jumped into the mud and ran up the path, urging the animals to follow. The bull pushed the female up the bank and followed. She scooped the Jungle Lord up with her trunk and put him back with Helene.

The pachyderms marched up the slippery hill to higher ground. Water fell by the barrelful. Lightning and thunder crashed around them. By nightfall, the storm had passed. It took days for the water to recede, but the elephant pair stayed until Ki-Gor and Helene were safe.

The journey down river was difficult. The River Congo was lined with broken trees and piled rocks. Ki-Gor and Helene picked their way carefully, at times traveling only a few miles per day. They helped villagers clear away wreckage and Ki-Gor hunted game to share.

A week into the journey home, after helping out a village, the people rewarded Ki-Gor and Helene with a boat. The couple made their way down river slowly and helped all in need.

As they passed through a flattened village, Helene said, "Ki-Gor, stop."

"What's wrong, my love?" Ki-Gor asked.

"I'm not sure, but something is odd there," Helene said. She pointed at a row of smashed huts. A tree trunk seemed to have flattened them.

Ki-Gor steered the boat to shore and they got out. Helene went over to the long, smoothly finished log. Ki-Gor followed.

"It's some kind of pole or something," Helene said.

The pair walked along it for twenty paces. Along the way, Ki-Gor fingered a few metal straps and rings fastened to the wood. "Men made this," Ki-Gor said.

At the far end of the pole were fractured boards attached by iron fittings. Helene looked at it a long time. Ki-Gor watched his wife as she knew far more of the ways of man.

She pondered a few minutes, and then smiled in disbelief. "It's the mast of a ship. A big one, too. Maybe 60 feet, judging by length of the mast."

"How did a ship that big get this far up river?" Ki-Gor wondered.

"I have no idea. But this wood very, very old," Helene said.

The Nordic girl was crafty, that much was clear to the man known simply as the Jackal. He had her briefly, but she got away before he had secured her. His two companions finally caught her scent after a day's search. He was sure that she couldn't be far.

His journey to the Congo was a long one, propelled by rumors and myth. Long before he was the Jackal, young Matthäus Lang fled to Africa after the Great War to avoid the horrid oppression of Germans throughout Europe.

He blended in with a Dutch crew on a freighter and jumped ship in Cairo. After overhearing some Egyptologists discuss a find they had made far south of the Valley of the Kings, Lang headed to the southern reaches of the Sahara. There he searched for the unopened tomb of Pharaoh Al Hasamedes, an early ruler, said to be rich with gold and artifacts. He was jumped by thieves in the night and left for dead, deep in the desert.

Lang barely survived the night and staggered across the sand for days. One night he awoke in the light of the full moon to the sound of barking in the dunes, not far away. He could barely move, but his hunger drove him toward the animals. The barks led him across the dunes until he spied a small oasis. He quenched his thirst and passed out. The next morning he was awakened by the sound of yipping and growls.

He opened his eyes to the sight of a recently mangled bird lying dead in front of him. Farther on, in the brush, was the source of the squeaky growls. Ignoring them for now, Lang looked at the bird. Desperately starving, he ripped the feathers off and ate it. Still on all fours, he drank from the small pool.

He had been searching for treasure, but hidden in that small oasis, he found something that served him far better than ancient trinkets. In the scrubby brush, barely surviving at the edge of the oasis he found two tiny pups. They were nearly starved, but they had saved him. He thought they were dogs and repaid the favor. He killed a snake and shared it with them. They followed him out of the desert and into his future.

As the pups grew older, he learned they were not dogs, but were spotted hyenas. By then, he was too attached and they were too tame to live on their own. They became his traveling companions.

He trained the sisters well and named them Furcht and Schicksal. Fear and Destiny. They were smart and cunning. With his ruthless reputation and the sisters tagging along, Lang earned his nickname, the Jackal.

It took many years to return to Africa and by then the hyenas were grown and had become one of the Jackal's most potent weapons. He had first heard the story in Copenhagen. It sounded crazy, but he followed it halfway around the world. He doubted his sanity. Then he found it in an antiquities shop in Johannesburg. Half a shield made of ancient iron and Iroko wood. The words "Vann Evig Liv" were carved into it in Old Norse. The shop owner claimed it was recovered from the wreck of a Portuguese cargo ship off the Western Coast of Africa at the turn of the century. The Jackal left with the artifact and shopkeeper was never seen again.

The Jackal took a freighter north to the African lumber capital, Boma, located on the Congo River delta in the Belgian Congo. The city was bustling and frontier wild. The Jackal felt right at home. When in town, he kept the hyenas on a leash. He showed the shield to a few of the old-timers, veterans of the lumber wars. They said upriver, way up river, were rumors of a race of white Africans. Their writing was described to look like that on the shield.

The Jackal hired a boat and went up river with his dogs as far as they could go. Then, they set off on foot. They hiked and climbed another two weeks through the jungle following the river ever upward.

Then he saw her through the trees, a blonde vision stripping off her boots, armor and helm. When she was the picture of natural beauty, she dove into a crystal clear pool in a spot where the river slowed. Her perfect, unadorned, alabaster skin knifed into the water.

The dogs were sent hunting while the Jackal moved in. He sat on a rock near her garments. Unlike the girl, the Jackal was dressed in boots, helmet, short pants, and a cotton shirt. Both the shirt and shorts had more pockets than a dozen kangaroos. He pulled off his pack. His compact machine gun dangled loosely around his neck.

Jackal was an efficient killer, comfortable with gun, knife, or garrote. He had at least one of each within easy reach. He relaxed and enjoyed the view as the sun glistened off the sparkling pool. Monkeys chattered in the trees and beautiful birds preened at the waters edge, drinking.

The girl swam about the pool, unaware of the Jackal's presence. She floated on her back and washed her straight blonde hair. The Jackal enjoyed the natural beauty. He hadn't seen a woman in months, much less a beauty in her state of undress.

She finally finished her washing and dove deep under the water. The Jackal lost sight of her among the rocks and his attention drifted back to a white ibis drinking at the river's shore.

After a few minutes he realized that it had been a long time since he had seen the blonde. He looked in the pool and then up and down the shore. She was gone.

Before he could call Furcht and Schicksal, he felt a sharp point in his back. He turned his neck. The young woman stood behind him. She held her sword to his spine, and looked none too pleased with him. He didn't realize how tall she was until she stood there, towering over him.

The Jackal smiled warmly and said, "Guten Tag, meine ich nicht schaden." The woman swung her sword and his world went black.

A grayness slowly materialized and the Jackal felt something warm and wet on his neck. He reached for it and expected to feel the sticky warmth of blood. The sensation of fur surprised him and his mind focused. He opened his eyes and saw Furcht. He smiled, but that made his head throb.

Furcht and Schicksal sniffed the air. They both growled and looked at their master, snarling with death in their eyes. They strayed off the trail and into the thick of the hot jungle. The Jackal stumbled to his feet and followed.

After fighting their way through miles of dense tropical forest, Jackal and his girls crested a hill and looked down toward the river.

The young Nordic woman marched down the path.

The Jackal tapped the sisters on the shoulder and said, "Gehen."

The pair silently raced down the hill toward the girl. She would not surprise them again, now it was their turn.

Furcht and Schicksal bounded down the hill and leaped at the girl. She whirled and swung her sword at them. Schicksal twisted out of the way, but the blade grazed her. The pair of hyenas circled the girl. They snarled and barked. She swung her sword again and they scattered, only to circle back. The girl flailed the sword wildly. She used it as a shield against the dogs.

The hyenas snapped at her. Then came the master.

The Jackal rushed down the path his pets had taken. The mercenary was in full kit; helmet, armored jacket, boots. His unusually sighted Mauser took aim, but didn't fire.

The woman swung her sword viciously at the sisters. They twisted and escaped the sword's bite. The girl turned and ran. She got a few seconds head start. The mercenary whistled at the hyenas and they reluctantly gave up the chase.

The Jackal knew that between him and his animals they would have no trouble tracking her.

The vines and branches of the jungle always provided Ki-Gor with a swift means of transportation away from the dangers below. Since boyhood, the Jungle Lord had swung fearlessly from tree to tree. He taught Helene all he knew, but she still had trouble keeping up.

It was not surprising that a girl who was raised in New York society and attended the finest schools could not keep up with the jungle man. What was surprising was how well she did. Helene was fearless and could follow Ki-Gor just about anywhere he went, but she was simply not as fast.

Ahead, a woman screamed. Ki-Gor grabbed a vine in mid-air and swung toward the screams. He kicked out at the end of his swing and flew to the next branch. He grabbed it and headed along through the tree routes. He looked back and barely saw Helene in the distance.

The screams were still ahead, but Ki-Gor saw a strange sight below him. There was a man, far too overdressed for the jungle, who ran a distance behind two spotted hyenas. The animals neared a woman that Ki-Gor couldn't quite see through the trees. The hyenas were large, fierce looking animals.

Ki-Gor leapt through the air and grabbed a branch at the last minute before he swung down onto the animals. The jungle man hit Furcht with a flying tackle. They tumbled in a ball that crashed into Schicksal. The melee began. Fist and might battled tooth and claw. Schicksal got her teeth into the jungle man's shoulder, but a blow to her head forced a retreat. Ki-Gor's mighty legs threw Furcht into a tree. She yelped and crumpled in a heap. The Jungle Lord dove onto the other sister.

"That will be quite enough!" The Jackal spat. Ki-Gor turned to see the man had leveled a machine gun at him. The Jackal gestured to the hyenas and said, "Lay another hand on my girls and I will kill you."

Ki-Gor released Schicksal. She paced between the Jackal and the Jungle Lord. "Why are you chasing that girl?" Ki-Gor asked.

Ki-Gor saw he had surprised the man.

"Who are you?" the Jackal said.

"I am Ki-Gor, Lord of the Jungle, protector of these lands. If you are wise, you will leave these lands while your animals still live."

Helene kept to the tree routes and passed Ki-Gor and the Jackal below. Helene sped ahead to see what had happened to the stranger's quarry. She soon caught up with the blonde woman. The former pilot swung down from the trees and landed in front of the girl.

The blonde intruder slid to a stop.

Helene said, "Are you alright?"

The young woman eyed Helene warily. "What thee want?" she said.

"To help you. Why was that man chasing you?"

The Nordic blonde turned away, "I need no help." She continued her march down the path.

Helene chased her and said, "Slow down, that man won't get you, Ki-Gor will see to that."

The girl kept walking.

Helene pursued, "Please wait, we can help." She softly put her hand on the blonde's shoulder.

The stranger whirled suddenly and unsheathed her blade. "I need no help, but it appears that you do." She swung the sword and Helene ducked just in time.

Helene was far from helpless. She stood up and circled around, blocking the blonde's path. The Nordic woman swung her sword, but the blow missed and dug into the soft earth.

Helene pounced on the sword arm and grasped the hilt tightly. She put her full weight on it. The young woman dropped the sword and Helene fell to the ground.

The Norse girl kicked Helene in the solar plexus. The blow knocked the wind out of her. The girl reached down to grab the sword. Helene grabbed her by the collar of her breastplate and pulled hard. The young woman fell to the ground.

Helene rolled on her and punched her across the jaw. Helene went to punch her again when she felt something wasn't right. The Nordic girl was too round around the middle.

Helene leaped off her and exclaimed, "You're…"

This took the girl by surprise. "What?" she said and rolled over. She grabbed the sword and got to her feet.

She looked at Helene and a rage came over her. The girl shrieked, "You must die!"

The Nordic girl charged Helene. The sword sliced through the air.

Helene dodged just in time. She felt the air whisper at the side of her head. The blonde came around again. Another strike just missed the aviatrix.

Helene kicked the sword and it flew out of the young woman's hand. Helene snatched it up and held it at the ready.

The blonde girl looked at the redhead armed with her own sword. It was too much, it was all too much. She collapsed to the ground and cried.

Helene stood a few paces off and let her cry. It took a moment for Helene to catch her breath, but when she did, she realized she had lost track of her mate. She looked back down the trail and softly said, "Ki-Gor." She dropped the sword and ran in pursuit.

The hyenas flanked their master. They emitted a low growl that drew attention to their sharp teeth. The Jackal looked at the blonde haired jungle man and remembered a newspaper article he read in Cairo. It was a wedding announcement that told about a boy that grew up in the jungle and survived on his wits. The article said he married some New York society skirt that had crashed her plane in the jungle and decided to go native.

Well, he didn't want to stir up trouble and attention by killing the local hero. The Jackal was a realist and a survivor. Killing Ki-Gor would cause far more trouble than it was worth and he needed to find the blonde girl before she vanished.

Cutting off a few precious feet of rope, he tied Ki-Gor to a tree. The mercenary was confident the rope and his pets could hold the jungle man long enough for him to escape. He whistled to get the hyenas attention and said, "Girls. Stay. Guard."

The animals turned their attention to Ki-Gor and showed him that they meant business.

"They are very well trained," Jackal said. "I would stay very still, if I were you. I'd hate to see you hurt."

The Jackal turned and ran up the trail, letting his precious pets guard the man.

Ki-Gor tested the sisters. He tried to loosen the ropes, but they yapped loudly and lunged at his legs.

The Jungle Lord sighed and considered his options. He didn't want to kill the animals as he had yet to figure out Jackal's angle. What was he after? An hour later, the hyenas' ears perked up. They snarled at Ki-Gor one last time and dashed off up the trail.

The Jackal ran. He could keep up the pace for miles, even with a heavy load of gear. He crested a hill and caught sight of Helene alone on the trail.

The soldier of fortune slowed down to a walk because he had just seen what Helene had missed. A pair of footprints veered off the path to the right ahead of him and headed up toward the plateaus that rose above the river.

Jackal looked back and saw his pets catching up. Afraid they would give away the trail leading off into the jungle, he called them to him.

Unfortunately, this drew the attention of the aviatrix. He didn't want her to see that he knew where the Nordic girl had gone, so he continued on the trail.

"Greetings fellow traveler," he said with a smile as he approached. "My name is Matthäus Lang, and you are?"

"Helene Kilgore."

"We are travelling the same way." He gestured at the hyenas and said, "Perhaps I could offer you some protection." The animals behaved themselves and flanked the party.

Helene eyed the man and his beasts warily. "Why were you chasing the girl?"

The Jackal laughed, "We had an argument and she wouldn't listen to reason. She is my sister."

"Your sister?" Helene blurted out.

The man smiled and nodded.

Helene asked, "Where did you come from?"

"Northern Germany."

The Jackal eyed the lovely Helene, barefoot in the jungle, wearing nothing but two tiny strips of leopard skin and pointedly asked, "Did you actually fly your plane, or were you just a passenger?"

"Oh I flew the plane, all right. I am… Well, I used to be a pilot."

"Fascinating," the mercenary said with a warm smile, but he was thinking that he better not underestimate this woman.

Helene asked, "Where is Ki-Gor?"

"He raced ahead of me, flying through the trees," the Jackal said.

Helene turned and walked down the narrow trail. The Jackal followed. They walked until nightfall.

The morning rays filtered through the leaves and woke Helene in her makeshift platform high in a tree.

She dropped to the ground and found herself alone. She searched the ground and found the Jackal's trail on a winding path through the wet jungle. She could see the effects of the storm still lingered. The animals were nervous and any game trails that had been there prior to the storm had washed away. She climbed over fallen trees and slogged through mud. Helene pushed ahead, driven by the need to find the girl. She trusted Ki-Gor would find her.

The morning sun illuminated a rope bridge that stretched across a tremendous chasm. Ki-Gor estimated that the distance across must be fifty steps or more. He adjusted the bow on his back and looked at the bridge.

Wooden slats were woven into the ropes that stretched out before him. He set his foot on the boards and pressed down. Solid. The wood was smooth on his bare feet, worn through years of use. Ki-Gor had never been this far up the Congo and there were no maps of the region. He wondered

…Jackal didn't want to hit the bridge…so he sent in the dogs.

who had built the bridge, and for that matter, when.

He stepped onto the bridge wondering how far ahead the Jackal and his dogs were. They had surely been across, as the hyena prints had led him to this spot. The mercenary was skilled, but couldn't hide his trail completely from Ki-Gor, the Jungle Lord.

The bridge swayed as he crossed. The wooden slats creaked in the rope. The gorge below was shrouded by an early morning mist. It was very deep, a hundred feet or more. The river was barely visible below and dotted with jagged pieces of rock that had fallen from the canyon walls.

Nearly half the massive span had passed under Ki-Gor's bare feet when his honed instincts noticed a faint vibration in the bridge. He ducked as he turned and two pistol shots cracked and echoed in the canyon. Ki-Gor saw the Jackal aim again and went flat. That stopped the shooting. His bow dug into his back.

The Jackal didn't want to hit the bridge with gunfire, so he sent in the dogs. They charged forward. Ki-Gor took off in a sprint.

The bridge shook wildly and that slowed down the hyenas. They looked nervously back at the Jackal. He urged them on, but the animals sensed that he didn't feel too safe either. He stopped scolding them and crossed as fast as he could, but Ki-Gor was out-pacing them. The Jungle Lord's feet slapped the bridge.

As Ki-Gor passed the mid-point of the span, a board splintered under Ki-Gor's foot and his leg went plunging through the bridge. As he fell, he grabbed wildly at the bridge. More boards crumbled from the impact. The Jungle Lord fell through and grabbed a rope beneath the bridge.

The Jackal smiled ruefully and picked up the pace. He hoped to catch the blond man while he dangled helplessly. His running caused the bridge to undulate wildly. It moved up and down in an unpredictable wave. Furcht and Schicksal got nervous and froze on the spot and made themselves as low as possible. Their master pressed on.

The ancient rope tore the skin of Ki-Gor's hands as he held on. He gritted his teeth in a snarl and forced his body up, using the swaying of the bridge in his favor. He held fast as the bridge swayed low, and then as it rose he took advantage of the force to help him up. Unfortunately, the bow slung on his back caught the rope and planks and kept him from getting back through the hole to the top of the bridge. With a heavy heart he squirmed out of the quiver and bow. They fell to the river.

The Jackal approached quickly. Ki-Gor saw him through the planks from under the bridge. He knew he had to get back on the bridge or he was a goner. He positioned himself under the broken section. Ki-Gor felt the undulating rhythm once more. When he reached an upward peak he let go. The force shot him through the broken planks into the air. He landed on his feet with the broken section of the bridge at his back and the Jackal was upon him.

One punch, then two, slammed Ki-Gor's midsection. Ki-Gor countered with an elbow to the face and the Jackal staggered back. He snarled at the jungle man and charged. Ki-Gor leaped off the side of the bridge, grabbed the rope handrail, and swung around behind the soldier of fortune and kicked him in the back as he returned to the bridge.

The force of the kick slammed the Jackal back toward the hole broken in the slats. The mercenary panicked and tried to leap past it, but he mistimed the jump because of the wild swaying and only his chest and arms made it across. His hands clawed the smooth worn wood and finally caught hold. His legs dangled beneath the bridge.

The hyenas were spurred on by the danger to their master. They were wary of the swaying and moved carefully across the bridge. The Jackal pulled at the slats and Ki-Gor jumped on his back. The combined weight was too much and the slats under the Jackal gave way.

They fell beneath the bridge, but each man managed to grab something. Ki-Gor caught a shattered slat. It hung on by a thin piece of ancient rope. The Jackal grabbed Ki-Gor's hair and dangled behind the Jungle Lord. The board in Ki-Gor's hand slowly slipped out of the rope. Beneath the bridge, Ki-Gor grabbed the unbroken slat ahead of him just as the broken one in his other hand came free.

Ki-Gor hung under the bridge. He elbowed and kicked, but he couldn't dislodge the mercenary on his back. With a massive effort, he moved hand over hand until he was well past the broken section.

The Jackal pulled a knife out his boot and stabbed it into Ki-Gor's shoulder. The Jungle Lord screamed and shook violently, trying to jar the man loose. The mercenary had his fingers intertwined in Ki-Gor's hair and held on.

Ki-Gor stopped his forward progress and let go with one arm. He held it off to his side and spoke through gritted teeth. "See this hand? If you don't get that knife out of my back I will let go with the other one and I guarantee that you will be dead before we hit the river."

The Jackal couldn't help looking down. The view was dizzying and far below the river was littered with granite shards. They glittered in the sunlight. The Jackal lost a bit of his nerve, then.

The best predator in the Congo sensed that the killer on his back was having second thoughts. Ki-Gor worked his way to the edge of the bridge. Then he slowly pulled himself up. Ki-Gor's head almost touched the bridge slats above.

The knife was firmly still in his back; the white-hot pain had not abated in the least. He chanced a look up. Furcht and Schicksal snarled at him through the slats.

Ki-Gor grimaced back at the hyenas and let go.

The men dropped nearly two feet before Ki-Gor grabbed the ropes at the side of the bridge. The Jackal was broken. He could barely breathe and the height was getting to him.

The Jackal pleaded, "Stop! Stop. Don't do that again." He looked at Ki-Gor's hands on the support rope.

Ki-Gor let go of the frayed rope with one hand.

The Jackal's eyes went wide. His eyes darted to Ki-Gor's other hand and watched a finger release the rope. "Come, on. Pull us up!" he said. Real panic was in his voice as he watched Ki-Gor's hand, mesmerized.

The Jungle Lord said, "The knife." The next finger lifted. Then the thumb relaxed its grip. Ki-Gor held on with just his index and middle fingers.

The Jackal tightened his hold on Ki-Gor's hair and pulled on the knife in Ki-Gor's back. Fresh blood poured out of the wound all over the knife. The mercenary's fingers slipped on the blood.

"I can't get a good grip!" he said, panicked.

"You better."

The Jackal shot a glance up and saw Ki-Gor briefly lift his index finger. The Jungle Lord said, "My fingers are getting really tired."

"I'm trying, I'm trying." The mercenary wrapped his fingers around the knife and tugged. The blade came free, but one of his fingers was cut deeply.

"Gaahhh," the Jackal said and dropped the knife. He grabbed Ki-Gor's hair with both hands.

"You're halfway there," Ki-Gor said. "Now the gun."

The Jackal unstrapped the machine gun and it plunged into the river.

Ki-Gor said, "The other one, too."

The custom Mauser with the black light scope came out of the holster. The Jackal felt the familiar grip and hated to lose it, but down it went. It took a long time to hit the water.

Ki-Gor said, "Grab the bridge!"

The Jackal reached up but the slats were too far away. "It's too far."

"Call off the dogs," Ki-Gor said. The order was quickly followed. The hyenas retreated. Ki-Gor pulled himself up. One arm grabbed the bridge; the other hoisted up his attacker.

The Jackal grabbed the slats and ropes and Ki-Gor let him go. The blonde jungle man swung up onto the bridge and started running. The Jackal pulled himself up and yelled for the hyenas. They raced past him toward Ki-Gor.

Ki-Gor looked back and then ahead. He figured he might reach the end of the bridge -- about fifty feet more -- just barely before the hyenas could slash through his Achilles tendons. He looked back. It was going to be close, he thought. Then he looked forward again.

There, at the end of the swaying rope bridge, was the blonde girl. She was at least his height and cut a striking figure with the tall boots, bare legs, fit stomach muscles, full chest... Then he saw it.

"Noooo!" he yelled. But it was too late.

She swung the battle-axe like a seasoned warrior. Her first swing cut the support lines on the right. The bridge swayed halfway over.

Ki-Gor grabbed the left support line and held tight. He swung there with the slats dangling down, swaying wildly below his feet. He turned back to see the hyenas falling, falling, falling to the river. He didn't watch long enough to see their fate. He looked to their master.

The Jackal held tight. He looked at the Nordic girl. She glared at him and let the two men dangle there a good minute and then shouted, "Die, smerige indringers."

The Jackal raced hand over hand back toward the other side.

The girl raised the battle-axe again and held it high.

"Stop!" Shrieked a shrill voice from across the river. It was Helene. She stood at the other end of the bridge. Her face was white as a sheet. Ki-Gor could see she was out of breath in addition to being terrified. He moved toward the girl as fast as he could.

The Jackal was headed toward Helene, in a few dozen yards he could start to use the edges of the slats to speed his progress.

Then the she-warrior swung the battle-axe down in a powerful stroke. The heavy razor sharp axe sliced through the full two-inch diameter of the ancient rope. The rope was severed, the wooden supports splintered, and the Nordic girl watched her problems fall to earth.

The bridge dropped like a pendulum. Ki-Gor's end of the line accelerated at terminal velocity toward the granite wall. He quickly decided that he would rather face the river than the cold, heartless stone wall. He aimed for a watery stretch clear of rocks and leaped into the air.

The girl turned away.

The Jackal weaved his arms and legs through the rope and braced for impact. He had scrambled back as far as he could to lessen the force of the inevitable collision.

The Jackal hit the unyielding stone with a massive slam that dislocated his left shoulder and might have broken his left leg. His head was ringing from the impact, but his helmet absorbed most of the force. He was fortunate that he was not farther down the bridge.

The Jungle Lord, on the other hand, had spent a lifetime swinging on vines through the forest and timed his jump into the river perfectly. His release put him right over the center of the river in a clear spot. He hit the water feet first and knifed down, down, down. The rains had raised the water level considerably and that alone probably saved Ki-Gor's life.

His powerful legs hit bottom and pushed back up. When he broke the surface, Helene whooped with joy. He looked far up the chasm and smiled to her.

The Jackal watched in horror as his beloved Furcht and Schicksal paddled helplessly against the might of the swollen river. Then they disappeared from sight and he knew that it wouldn't be long before they reached the falls that cascaded into that beautiful lake. He started climbing.

Ki-Gor's muscles strained against the river's might. Shoulders and legs pushed harder than they had ever pushed before. Finally, as Ki-Gor came near the rivers' edge, the current eased. The end of the bridge dangled a few feet above the water. Ki-Gor grabbed it and pulled himself up out of the raging river.

A scream forced his eyes upward. The Jackal was gone and Helene must be alone with the man. Ki-Gor climbed the bridge like a ladder. His shoulder complained, but he'd suffered worse.

Helene had screamed only once, but Ki-Gor's imagination got the best of him. He had seen much of the dark face of human nature. Slavers, killers, cannibals -- the deep wilds of Africa had much to offer in the way of human suffering.

His arms felt like lead weights. His shoulder throbbed from the stab wound. Ki-Gor was two thirds of the way up the cliff face when there was another scream. A man's this time. Ki-Gor smiled knowing that Helene was still alive. That knowledge renewed his energy. He climbed.

When he neared the top, Helene peeked over the side. She smiled broadly and looked back over her shoulder and said, "He's coming." Then she looked back to Ki-Gor and urged him on, "It's not too much farther. Almost there."

Ki-Gor reached her and she helped him up over the edge of the cliff. He collapsed to the ground and Helene was on him, kissing his lips and stroking his hair.

She looked deep into his eyes and said, "I don't think I have been that scared since I crashed my plane."

Ki-Gor smiled at her. He looked around and sat up, his expression souring. "Where is he? He didn't hurt you, did he?"

"No." She was grinning.

"You screamed."

Helene laughed. "His shoulder was dislocated. When he popped it back in it made a quite disgusting sound."

Ki-Gor stood, chest still pumping. "Where is he?"

"I sent him away for a few minutes. I thought that would be for the best."

Ki-Gor was surprised. "You... Sent him. And he went."

"Yes. I was afraid that you might... well, hurt him," she said.

"I've had worse." Ki-Gor pushed her off him and stood up. "He tried to kill me, you know."

"I'm not so sure about that. He could have shot you."

"He tried," Ki-Gor said.

"But I don't think he really meant it. I mean, I think there has been some misunderstanding and you really should hear him out."

Ki-Gor turned around and showed her the shoulder wound. "I think he was serious."

Helene's jaw dropped. She stammered out, "How..."

Ki-Gor said, "Happened under the bridge."

"The river cleaned it out pretty well," Helene said. Her eyes darted around the jungle and settled on a low, thick leaved plant. She ran to it and snapped off one of the leaves. A thick greenish fluid oozed from the break. Helene smeared it heavily on the wound. "Your friend N'geeso taught me the land has many resources."

Ki-Gor smiled and said, "He is very wise. Thank you. Now, we need to catch that girl." He looked up the trail. In the distance another plateau rose up ahead of them. An easy way up did not present itself. From where they were, the sheer wall climbed vertically at least a thousand paces to the summit. A majestic waterfall seemed to flow out of heaven, as the top of the plateau was shrouded in fog.

The rock face was not utterly barren, however. There were vines and creepers and even a few small trees that somehow managed a to cling to the granite wall. Secondary waterfalls poured water down as well, although they were a trickle compared to the main branch of the Congo.

Ki-Gor sensed movement behind him and turned to face the Jackal.

The man said, "I am not expecting you to like me, but I would like you to help me find my sister."

"I'll find her, but she is not your sister," Ki-Gor said. "I'm not sure what she is, but I intend to find out." He looked at the Jackal and said, "I'm not sure what you are either, but I doubt you'll tell me. You seem to be a survivor more than anything. Why do you chase the girl?"

The question took the man off guard. Helene looked at him pointedly. Ki-Gor waited. The fight on the bridge and the dizzying climb had taken the lies out of the Jackal and at that moment Matthäus Lang was standing on the trail, not sure what to say.

He said, "I think she is part of a Nordic outpost somewhere up river, and I am going to find them."

Helene was skeptical. "What makes you think that?"

The Jackal opened his rucksack and pulled out the fragment of shield. He said, "This was found many years ago floating off the African coast just west of the Congo River delta."

Helene looked at the wooden fragment; her fingers ran over the carved rune-like writing. Her mind went to the ship's mast she had found with Ki-Gor In the village down river. The writing was the same. The wood was the same.

The redhead said, "Ki-Gor, he could be right. She could be a Viking maiden. She certainly looks like one, but she needs help. I talked to her. She is just a frightened girl."

"A frightened girl with a big axe. We should be careful," the Jackal said. "We go then, I will fight you no longer." He thrust out his hand to Ki-Gor and said, "At least not today."

Ki-Gor looked at the hand a moment and then shook it. He smiling at the man and said, "Good enough."

Then Ki-Gor turned and headed toward the monolithic wall of rock rising up to the sky. The next plateau. He knew not of Vikings and ships, but he knew Helene wanted to help the girl and that was enough. He would keep a close eye on this man, this tamer of jackals. He was not a man to be trusted.

A tiny splinter of rock was the only handhold that Ki-Gor could find. He reached for it, his body stretched to its limits. He got three fingers on it and pulled himself up. A slightly larger hold was above. Ki-Gor grabbed it with his other hand.

The rock tore away from the cliff face. "Look out!" the Jungle Lord yelled, clawing for another grip. Down below, Helene and the Jackal ducked their heads as the rock careened past.

"Nice try, jungle man, but you missed," the Jackal said.

The climb to the second plateau had been very difficult. Much of the time the Jackal's climbing ropes had to be used, with Ki-Gor leading the way.

When they reached the summit, the Jungle Lord pointed into the distance at a high waterfall that flowed from the third, and highest, plateau. He said, "There. The Plateau of the Gods. Our destination. The rumored home of the white Africans. They are said to dwell along the river Congo. It is also said that the mesa is the source of the Congo itself."

Helene looked upon the distant plateau rising majestically above them and wished she had her plane. The vertical rise must top four thousand feet, but fortunately it did not look completely vertical. It would be difficult, but they could climb it. First however, they had to face the jungle.

The trek through the jungle was incredibly difficult. On more than one occasion the Jackal stopped and spent valuable time and energy cursing the universe for sending him to such a miserable place.

The perils were many. The Jackal looked up in the trees and marveled at Ki-Gor and Helene making better time than he did on the ground. Helene took a leap off a branch fifty feet in the air and spent a few seconds in flight before she grabbed a flexible branch that sprung her to another branch and so on.

"The tree routes," was what the Jungle Lord and his mate called it. The Jackal thought it looked like suicide perpetually postponed. On the other hand, the terrestrial path invited fire ant bites, wild boar attacks, and a narrowly avoided leopard attack.

Ki-Gor convinced the mercenary that he should at least sleep in the trees. The journey to the Plateau of the Gods took three days, but they finally reached the base of the monolithic plateau and made camp for the night.

After Helene made up their arboreal accommodations, the Jackal roasted some antelope on a small fire. The meal was quiet and after filling their bellies, Ki-Gor and Helene professed exhaustion and retired for the night in the nest Helene had made in the trees.

The Jackal sat alone by the fire, but he was more exhausted than he thought and soon fell asleep.

Warm, wet kisses filled the Jackal's dreams. He smiled and wondered who the lady was. He slowly awoke and discovered the kisses were real. It was black as pitch. The Jackal had fallen asleep in front of the fire. A soft orange glow told him where the flames had been.

A soft wet tongue pushed up against his face and the Jackal smiled. He spoke softly, to not arouse the jungle couple that slept overhead. "Schicksal? Furcht?" he said.

The animals nuzzled him and pushed him down. The three wrestled and he rubbed their bellies and stroked their heads.

Stark sunlight crested the top of the Plateau of the Gods and beat down on the jungle couple. Ki-Gor forced his eyes open and saw the sun was already high in the sky.

"Damn," he said and roused his wife.

Helene rolled over and rested her head on his chest. She was still half asleep.

"What's the trouble, dear?" she yawned.

"It is nearly noon. We have slept the morning away."

Helene sat upright and said, "Oh my God, you're right."

Ki-Gor rubbed his head and said, "I feel groggy."

"Yeah, me to," Helene said and rolled back over.

Ki-Gor grabbed her. "No!" he said.

"Leave me alone, I'm tired," she said, putting her head down.

"Get up," he said and pulled her to her feet. "I'll bet this is the work of that Jackal."

That jolted Helene awake. "He slipped us a Mickey, the rat." Her face glistened with sweat from the heat of the day.

The Jungle Lord stepped off the tree. Had any of Helene's old friends been there, they would have panicked at the sight of him falling 25 feet to the ground, but Helene didn't give it a second thought, like other wives calmly watched their husbands catch a subway tube.

Ki-Gor grabbed a passing branch and it slowed his fall. He released it and dropped the final ten feet to the ground. His mighty leg muscles, trained by a lifetime of survival in the wild, absorbed the weight of his fall and his bare feet landed softly on the ground by the fire. A hand over it told him it was long cold. He scanned the ground.

His wife slid down a vine and joined him. He looked at the ground and saw the hyena tracks.

"The Jackal's pets have returned to him and they are gone, probably half the day ahead."

"Then we run," Helene said.

Ki-Gor smiled and said, "And that is why I love you."

They bolted down the trail. Ki-Gor let Helene set the pace, though he took the lead. His quick reflexes and astonishing tracking ability let him follow the others, despite the Jackal's attempt to hide the trail. They ran up the slight grade toward the towering plateau ahead.

Ki-Gor followed the Jackal's trail. It was headed straight for the plateau. Whatever he was after was sure to be found there. But what was so important that a man like him, a soldier for hire, would trek across the globe and through the wilds of unexplored central Africa to find? The girl? He was already on the path to something before he met her. She was just a distraction. What did the girl and her people have?

They camped in the crook of a tree that night, nestled in each other's arms. They were on their way early the next morning and reached the plateau's thin shadow by noon the next day.

Helene looked at the massive wall of rock that rose up to the sky ahead of them and exclaimed, "There! Do you see it?" she pointed.

Ki-Gor followed her look and saw the three shapes moving slowly along the middle of the plateau's rock face, just above the tree line. "The Jackal," he snarled.

"And his furry friends. It looks like they are following a trail," Helene said.

The jungle got remarkably thicker as they entered the narrow zone where the plateau's shadow kept the sun's blasting rays from ever directly hitting the ground. It was merely a few hundred paces to the shattered rock face, but the ground was thick with creepers and vines, snakes, spiny trees, and thousands of insects.

Ki-Gor slashed his way through with his knife. He cursed, "Gods, this jungle is thick!"

He lost the Jackal's trail almost as soon as they entered the jungle due to the multitude of animal tracks that criss-crossed through the dense forest. The perpetual shade attracted thousands of animals. But tracking him hardly mattered, because he knew they would pick up his trail soon enough. The Jackal was headed to the Plateau of the Gods, and so were they.

Ki-Gor and Helene reached the base of the plateau. Monumental piles of rock that had broken off the cliff face blocked their progress. They skirted the edge for a time, looking for a way through.

After an hour, Helene said, "Ki-Gor, it's no use. If there is a path through, we may never find it." She pointed up at the winding, narrow path that ran along the side of the plateau. "Look, the path is there on the side of the mountain. Let's go."

"You are up to it?"

Helene shook her head, "Not really, but I don't see another choice."

Ki-Gor kissed her. "Over the rocks we go," he said. He took her hand and started across the enormous rocks left by eons of rockslides. As they slowly gained altitude they could see segments of a trail below them, but the path did not reveal itself. They kept climbing. The going was rough, but Helene proved she was tougher.

At times they needed to leap from one rock to the next. Helene practically ran to keep up with Ki-Gor. He moved with such natural grace that it looked like he was just out for a Sunday stroll.

They made their way up the slope to the trail. From then on they followed the switchbacks until they reached the summit.

They crested the final ridge and the Plateau of the Gods was spread out before them. They stood near the southwest corner of the rectangular table mountain.

A savage wind whipped their hair and snapped at the edges of their leopard hide clothing. A plain of bare rock covered a narrow region of the plateau.

Beyond the rocky wasteland, the vast remainder of the plateau was covered in jungle. They were on the highest part of the plateau and a huge lake was barely visible in the far distance. The recent storms filled the lake to overflowing, but there was no river to be seen, even though they knew it had to be there. The spectacular waterfall off the mountain was a testament to that.

They marched onward. Ki-Gor took the lead, watching for predators and searching for any sign of the Jackal. There was nothing. After an hour, grass and a few hardy trees broke up the rocky surface. Ki-Gor and Helene rested in the shade of one such tree for a few minutes and then moved on.

There was no stark line where the bare rock ended and the jungle began, but soon enough they were in the welcome shade and cool embrace of the forest.

Ki-Gor's eyes constantly scanned the ground and found the Jackal's trail. It started with a paw print. Then another. Then a careless boot print in a muddy patch. Once they had spotted it, Ki-Gor and Helene managed to follow the trail. It headed roughly east through the jungle.

After climbing through the huge roots of a mangrove tree, Helene caught sight of something odd. A second set of boot tracks. She smiled. "Ki-Gor. Look at this."

"He's tracking the blonde girl," Ki-Gor said.

Helene said, "We better hurry."

They increased the pace, fairly flying through the wild country now. Ki-Gor took the lead, and with four sets of tracks to follow, they could move fast. Fraught with worry for the maiden, Helene had no trouble keeping up.

Ki-Gor slid to a stop, grabbed Helene around the waist, and stopped her suddenly.

She asked sharply, "What? What is it Ki-Gor?"

He parted the branches of a low fern. Just ahead was a long, jagged, dark patch of ground twenty to thirty feet across. It ran across their path and stretched up and down the mesa into the distance.

Ki-Gor thought he might be able to jump across it, given a good running start, but he was sure it was too much for Helene. He put his finger to his lips in a request for silence. Helene complied. In the quiet they could hear the low whisper of a distant river.

"A black river?" Helene asked.

Ki-Gor did not answer the question. Instead he said, "Hold my feet."

Helene looked at him quizzically, but complied as he lay on his belly and pushed himself toward the darkness.

As Ki-Gor got closer he realized that this was not a river of blackness, but an illusion created in their minds. There was quite literally nothing there.

When he got close enough, he grasped a rocky edge and peered over. The sight was enough to cause his head to swim.

He took a long, slow breath and a whispered, "I think we have found the Gods alright."

"What are you talking about?" she said.

"Come look."

Helene crawled up next to him and she saw that the river had carved away the rock of the plateau leaving behind a most spectacular sight. A deep canyon had formed. It was narrow along the top, but as the water cut through the rock the canyon got wider and narrower, again and again, until it formed a series of horizontal rocky shelves; tiers that lined both sides of the canyon.

While the canyon was at times a mere twenty feet wide across the top, it widened to several hundred feet at the several points, then narrowed again until the river itself was fifty feet wide at the bottom. Upriver, Ki-Gor could see a waterfall cascading into the hidden canyon.

But the most amazing thing was what lined those long rock shelves; that was the sight that took their breath away.

There was a city built on the tiers. An ancient city made of wood and stone. There were homes and shops and taverns. And people. Hundreds of people.

They were a fair-haired lot, the people of the canyon. That much Ki-Gor and Helene could see from their vantage point.

She looked at her husband. "Vikings. A whole Viking village. Hidden from the world for ages. I wonder how they got here?" Helene said.

Ki-Gor looked at her. "Vikings? You use a word I do not know. What are Vikings?"

Helene thought carefully. "They are an ancient clan of people that lived in the North Country, far, far from here, where winter comes early and stays almost through summer. There, the nights are long and it is cold for months. Some Vikings lived in places that had ice on them year round. They believed in a pantheon of Gods that lived in a place called Asgard. The Vikings have been gone from our world a long, long time."

"Not these," Ki-Gor said.

Helene thought the Viking village looked a bit like a Nordic Mesa Verde. Buildings and ladders ran along the upper strata and small fields lined the ends of many of the tiers.

The buildings were ornate wood constructions with carved wood trim and open windows. It was a beautiful Nordic village, except that the Vikings had somehow sailed to central Africa and survived in this hidden valley for hundreds of years.

Men and women tended the fields, and people were chatting or climbing ladders between the strata of the city. A large wooden box, strung on stout ropes, was pulled from tier to tier like a cross between an elevator and aerial tram.

Near the river, a number of shouting blonde men with ropes and pulleys hoisted up a large water wheel that lay on the ground. Lighter colored wood revealed where the wheel had been recently repaired. One of the tall support beams also looked new.

The men got the wheel into place and the river went to work, turning the wheel. Water pushed the wheel around and was scooped up into buckets around the wheel. The water rode the wheel to the top and then dumped into an aqueduct several levels above the river. The men cheered.

"Helene," Ki-Gor said and pointed at a large building several tiers above the river. It was strange looking, with a long series of holes along the side and a wide wooden strip that ran the length of its curved roof. A slender woman surreptitiously entered the building through an open doorway in the side.

"That's her!" Helene said. "The girl. At least that Jackal didn't get her."

"There's something about that building..." Ki-Gor said. He rolled over onto his back and leaned his head over the precipice.

"What are you doing?"

Ki-Gor ignored her. He looked at the long rounded building upside down.

"A boat... That building is a boat," he said and rolled back over.

Helene smiled, "You're right. The windows running along the side are where the oars would stick out." But that's bigger than any Viking ship I ever heard of.

Ki-Gor's gaze went back to the water wheel in the river. He looked at the new support beam and said, "The water wheel. The supports for that are about as long as that log we found. The storm must have ripped it loose and it flattened that village downstream."

"The mast," Helene said. "They used the mast to support the water wheel."

Ki-Gor looked along the riverbank and realized that where once were many buildings, now were only ruins. The flood destroyed much of the settlement. He wondered how many lives were lost.

"Those people have suffered a great tragedy," Ki-Gor said.

"I wonder if that's why the girl is returning," Helene said.

"We must meet them before that Jackal taints their mind with his lies."

Helene thought the Viking village looked …like a Nordic Mesa Verde.

"Too late," Helene said, pointing down.

A pair of huge Viking warriors escorted the Jackal and his dogs to the ship-building. He looked more like a prisoner than a guest. His hyenas were caged outside and the Jackal was shoved through the doorway. Shouts went out and more sturdy Viking men filed into the ship-building.

Ki-Gor looked to the ends of the valley and saw that it was unlikely that they could enter to the North as the waterfall there was high above the canyon floor and any climb down that way looked impossible.

That left the southern end of the valley, where the river flowed out through a waterfall to the plateau below. They set off.

Ki-Gor and Helene followed the winding path down the stone cliff toward the river.

Spray from the falls kept the Southern end of the valley shrouded in fog. It also kept the rocks slippery.

Those algae soaked rocks almost took another victim when Helene stepped too hard on a slick rock. Her foot shot out from under her. She plunged past Ki-Gor. He snapped out a hand and caught her wrist just in time. He pulled her back onto the path and held her close. Her arms wrapped around him like a python.

He stood there and let her hold him. When enough time had passed, he gently separated their bodies and they continued down. Helene was more careful, because the closer they got to the falls, the more slippery it became.

Ki-Gor led the way, treading carefully down the slope. He saw a blonde sentry posted in a little nook below them. He turned to his wife and silenced her with a look. He held up a hand to keep her put and crept down alone.

His bare feet were silent on the stone path. His body was as taut as a coiled spring, ready to leap onto the guard at any moment. The guard hadn't moved. Ki-Gor wondered if he was asleep.

When he was just out of sword range, Ki-Gor picked up a pebble and tossed it down the path past the sentry. The stone clattered down the mountain trail. The guard still did not move.

Sound asleep, Ki-Gor thought. He crept up behind the Viking man.

Ki-Gor snapped his hand out and covered the man's mouth to stifle any scream. His hand snapped back just as quickly. The man's skin was ice cold.

Ki-Gor nudged the guard's chin and his head lolled so far back the man's helm fell off and clattered in the rocks. His head kept going back un-til it struck the man's own spine. The dead sentry's bushy beard concealed a bloody mess on his chest. Something had severed his throat and most of his spine in a clean wound.

Above him, Helene gasped loudly from the sudden shock of seeing the cross section of the Viking's neck. "Oh my God," she said.

"That mercenary is more dangerous than I thought," Ki-Gor said.

"I thought he was alright, not a friend, but decent, human. I guess that was just an act," Helene said. "He's an animal." She looked at the beheaded Norseman.

Ki-Gor warned, "He will poison them to us. We must be careful."

Helene couldn't take her eyes off the dead sentry. Grim faced, she looked at her husband and said, "I have an idea."

"I'm not sure I like the sound of that."

From the ground, the Valley of the Lost was spectacular, but the beauty was tempered by devastation from the flood. The Sentry pushed Helene along as they climbed over the timber, rubble and shattered trees block-ing the trail into the valley. The floodwaters must have reached fifty feet. There was a line of scum and debris that went midway across the remaining buildings of the first tier. Many of the structures along the riverbanks had been simply swept away.

The tiers rose up the canyon walls like slashes of paint on a canvas. Deep brown wood and green fields and the reds and oranges of sandstone were stacked up in layers of color. And at the top, in a jagged slash across the roof of the world, was the pure blue of the African sky.

The settlement was built up on both sides of the river valley. There was sugar cane, wheat, and barley growing in the fields along the tiers.

Across the river Helene saw men pulling bodies out of the debris that clogged the canyon. The smashed pieces of their lives were jammed against the river's exit and made the flooding all the worse.

Some of the men waved and shouted a greeting. Ki-Gor wore the dead Sentry's clothes and armor. He was pushing Helene along like she was a prisoner. Ki-Gor's neck and chest were covered with the Sentry's blood in a manner that simulated a severe neck wound.

Ki-Gor waved back at the men. He hoped that no one would talk to him, because he did not speak Old Norse and despite blending in visually, the disguise was truly superficial.

The pair quickly realized that the canyon was now divided. There was evidence that several bridges once crossed the river, but those had been destroyed. Small boats were being used in their place. The intruders would have to use one of the boats to get across and then climb several of the temporary ladders up to the third tier where the ancient ship rested upside-down.

The bloody Ki-Gor held a cloth soaked with crimson to his neck as the pair approached a boat.

The waiting boatman said, "Hva har skjedd med deg?"

Ki-Gor feigned choking noises and shoved Helene onto the boat. He climbed in and the boatman used a long pole to shove the small boat across the river.

Ki-Gor bowed in thanks to the boatman and dragged Helene roughly onto shore. He pushed her toward one of the ladders.

While they were climbing, Helene said, "Do you have to be so rough?"

"Just trying to be like them. Savage."

They reached the first tier and got a closer look at the devastation. The river had smashed through the outer streets, wiping them off the rock. The intruders could also see that the tiers went back much further than they had thought. There were at least three streets running parallel to the canyon.

Helene looked down a cross street deep into the tier and said, "The buildings are made of rock quarried out of the canyon. They made these tiers themselves."

"Or built upon what nature provided," Ki-Gor said.

They arrived at a ladder that reached up to the next level. It looked new. Once again, Ki-Gor grunted and prodded Helene to climb.

Helene gripped the ladder and went up. They reached the third tier. The streets of this level were more crowded with people. They hustled on their way. The flood didn't damage these streets as much as those below.

Ki-Gor and Helene were largely ignored as he led her to the overturned ship.

They eyed the shops, homes and taverns along the road. Helene was enthralled by the markets that were lined with clothes, armaments, and food. Oh, dear Lord, the food, she thought.

Ki-Gor shoved her on toward the overturned hull. The pedestrians stared at Helene with her leopard hide clothes and fiery red hair. Strangers were an uncommon sight.

They reached the overturned longship's hull. It was larger than they had imagined. It ran fully fifty paces long, was 10 paces wide and was at least eight long paces up to the top of the narrow keel.

They reached the main entrance. Ki-Gor pushed Helene through the opening and into the dark interior. For a moment, it was black as night inside. Their eyes adjusted and shapes began to appear in the dimly lit room.

The domed hull of the ship arched up high above them. Fires burned in braziers around the large open room. Wood and animal hide screens divided up the space. Woven rugs lined the polished stone floor.

Flood survivors filled most of the divided spaces. They were homeless, but looked healthy. They stared at the silent visitors. Ki-Gor made grunting noises and pointed at his neck and then at Helene.

A tall, thin, young Viking woman approached and asked, "Who is this woman? Why do you dare bring her here?"

Ki-Gor again feigned injury and struggled to make noises. The woman looked at him sternly. She pointed at the ground and said, "Wait here. I will be back with Bodvär."

The woman stalked off and disappeared behind a bamboo screen. Helene and Ki-Gor stood on the hide of a water buffalo and waited.

A booming voice said, "Svetlana! Who have you brought to me?"

Ki-Gor and his bride turned to see a mountain of a man behind them. He stood fully eight feet tall and had a shock of black hair that sprouted beneath his golden crown. A thick, braded beard flowed below his waist. He wore light armor and boots. The intruders were stunned; they stared openly at the giant Viking.

The King looked at Ki-Gor and scowled, "Silence? Is that anyway to treat Bodvär the Bold, King of the Lost Vikings, your gracious host?" Ki-Gor and Helene froze, looked at each other.

After beat, Bodvär laughed heartily and slapped Ki-Gor on the shoulder, nearly dislocating it. His jovial mood vanished when he noticed the armor Ki-Gor was wearing.

The King looked at the thin woman and said, "Get something to clean up that armor." She scurried away.

"Come!" he said harshly to the intruders. The King turned and walked deeper into the hull. Ki-Gor and Helene followed.

They reached the far end of the ship. A carved Dragon's head was mounted above a massive oak throne.

Beside the throne was a sturdy wooden stand holding a six-foot long battle-hammer and the King's Shield, a massive piece of brass and steel with ornate carvings. Animal skin cushions lined the floor and the king gestured for the visitors to sit.

Bodvär took his place at the throne. His hand casually rested on his huge battle-hammer. He said, "Visitors. We get them not often. Now, three in a week." That got their attention.

The woman returned with a bowl of water and towels. The massive king gestured to Ki-Gor. "Come now, modesty has no place here."

The woman removed the Jungle Lord's helmet, armor and his bloody clothing. She washed his face and neck. Helene watched her closely and gave her a warning glance. Ki-Gor was glad to be rid of the armor.

The Viking leaned toward them and asked, "How get you here, to this place?"

Ki-Gor said, "We walked. We followed…" Helene elbowed him sharply.

"Did you follow Freyrrun, my daughter, here?"

"The Viking girl is his daughter," Helene muttered to herself.

"No," Ki-Gor said. "We followed a man who took some… something from us."

"The hyena master?"

"Yes."

Bodvär the Bold stood upright, his towering presence dwarfing them. His voice was contained, soft, but Ki-Gor felt it fighting to scream. "What do you know of him?"

"Very little," Ki-Gor said. "We met him just a few days ago on the trail." The thought made him chuckle.

"What is so funny?" the King interrupted.

"He tried to kill me. More than once."

"And that is funny?" Bodvär asked without expecting an answer. He continued, "How is it that you came to kill my son?"

Helene was shocked and blurted out, "Your son? We have killed no one."

Bodvär was not used to being spoken to in such a manner. He pointed at the helmet and armor Ki-Gor wore and said, "Then how did thee come to wear his garb?"

The mighty king poked a finger the thickness of Helene's wrist into Ki-Gor's neck. "To defile his blood?"

Ki-Gor looked at the clothes and said, "We were trailing the Jackal and found a man dead at his post. We decided to…"

That was too much for the king. He swung in anger and struck Ki-Gor in the chest. The Jungle Lord flew far across the room and smashed through a bamboo divider.

The King of the Vikings was on him in three steps and yanked him from the wreckage.

Helene, forgotten for now, dashed off, looking for Freyrrun, the King's daughter. She was sure the girl must be here somewhere.

The Viking squeezed the Jungle Lord's chest with one hand. Ki-Gor felt the pressure building in his head and said, "I am not your enemy."

Bodvär threw him into the back wall and stalked forward to grab him again. Ki-Gor snatched up a bowl and threw it in the king's face. Then the Jungle Lord grabbed one of the ship's ribs and climbed. The king reached for him but missed. Ki-Gor kept climbing.

The wooden ribs arched to the center of the roof and Ki-Gor got quite a view of the King's Public House. He spotted the Jackal and the girl.

The mercenary shoved her to the ground and ran out a dark rear exit. She collapsed, sobbing on the ground.

"Helene!" Ki-Gor shouted.

"Ki-Gor?" she called.

She spotted him and he gestured toward the dark opening in the back of the ship. "The girl's there," he yelled.

Helene ran off and Ki-Gor turned his attention back to the Viking.

Bodvär returned to his throne and dropped to one knee. He placed his hands upon his battle-hammer and bowed his head. "Bjärkamal, Hammer of the Gods, I thank you for your service. We have made many journeys, and fought many foes. You travelled with me from Midgard to Valhalla and back. I request your service once more."

Bodvär the Bold lifted the hammer, Bjärkamal, high above his head.

The Jungle Lord felt something in the air, like a storm approaching. Down below, the Viking pointed the battle-hammer at Ki-Gor.

The Jungle Lord released the wooden beam and fell just before a bolt of lightning thundered out of the hammer. It blew a wide hole through the beam and roof and blasted the rocks above.

Ki-Gor hit the ground and smelled the ozone from the lightning. He wondered just what manner of man this Bodvär was. Clearly, he could not beat him in a fight.

Helene ran frantically through the strange building and did her best to ignore the exotic smells of the rich food and the allure of the beautiful and friendly people. She had to get to the daughter, Freyrrun. She had to convince the girl to stop her father before he killed Ki-Gor.

After a few wrong turns, Helene suddenly stopped. The King's daughter lay in a corner, sobbing.

The first CRACK! BOOM! of lightning and thunder startled them. Helene and Freyyrun both jumped at the sound and their eyes locked. The girl looked so scared. Helene knelt to the girl and held out her arms.

Freyrrun wrapped her arms around Helene and wept. CRACK! BOOM! went the lightning again and the girl flinched in her arms. Helene just held her tight and made soothing sounds.

The hole in the floor smoldered at Ki-Gor's feet. He jumped back and ran behind the massive oak chair, hoping the king would be loath to destroy his own throne.

While that was true, it didn't prevent the king from tossing it out of the way with a flick of his wrist. Ki-Gor was exposed again and Bjärkamal swung wildly at him.

The battle-hammer missed the leaping Jungle Lord and shattered a hole through the hull of the longship. Ki-Gor landed and grabbed the massive King's Shield from its hanger. Bodvär ripped the hammer from the wall and left a splintered opening.

Bodvär swung Bjärkamal again in his wild rage. Ki-Gor saw the Viking's emotions rise up. The Jungle Lord blocked with the shield and it cushioned the blow far more than he expected. He wasn't even pressed back by the attack.

Bodvär cursed, "Damn you! I shall send you to Valhalla for what you have done."

The furious King circled around and Ki-Gor moved until his back was to the opening ripped in the side of the ship. Ki-Gor hated to lose the shield, but it might provide him the moment of cover that would let him escape.

The Viking girl stopped crying and looked up at Helene and said, "Thank you."

Helene smiled at the young girl and said, "My pleasure."

The girl smiled faintly. "I don't even know your name."

"Helene."

The young girl said, "Thank you Helene. I am Freyrrun Bodvärsdotter, and I am in much danger."

"But your father is King," Helene said. Then she realized, "Oh. Ohhh. He doesn't know."

Freyrrun pushed Helene away. "How do you?"

Helene stroked the girl's cheek gently. "I felt it back in the jungle, when I tackled you."

"If he finds out I will die." She placed her hand on her belly and felt the child that was too small to show itself. "We will die."

"Why?"

"Because that is our way here." Freyrrun said. She looked pleadingly at Helene. "Please, take me with away with you. I am a good hunter."

CRACK! BOOM! The mighty Bjärkamal spoke again, and the world shook.

Freyrrun took the redheaded stranger's hand and stood, pulling her up. "Helene, we must go."

"Not until we find my husband," Helene said.

The wooden shard seemed long enough, Ki-Gor thought. He ducked through the jagged hole torn in the side of the hull and grabbed the piece of wood. He jammed it across the boards and through the arm straps of the King's Shield.

He hoped it would delay the King long enough for him to escape. Bjärkamal slammed against the shield and it held.

Ki-Gor ran. He hoped to circle around behind the ship-building and find another entrance to use to search for Helene.

Unfortunately for the Jungle Lord, the ship was pressed right up against the rock. He would have to find another way. He spotted a ladder and ran to it.

Helene and Freyrrun ran out of the building. Helene spotted Ki-Gor climbing a ladder with the King not far behind. She raced after them. Helene was reached the ladder and Freyrrun tried to stop her.

"Please, stop. We need to find that horrible man with the dogs," Freyrrun said.

Helene looked down at her, "Why is he so important? Who is he? Is he the father?"

The girl spat, "Don't disgust me. He killed my brother and he is a threat to our whole way of life. As are you."

Helene stopped and said, "Ki-Gor and I would never betray you to the outside world. Your people have done a good job of staying apart, hidden. We certainly had no inkling that this city even existed."

Helene turned and climbed. The girl reluctantly followed. They reached the top of the ladder and Helene looked out at the glorious vista of the Valley of the Lost. Pedestrians padded past behind them, speaking Old Norse. Helene looked for the men, but saw no sign of them.

The ladder swayed a bit as Ki-Gor climbed. As he reached the top, the ladder shook violently. Ki-Gor looked down and saw Bodvär. The Jungle Lord quickly scrambled over the top in fear that the mass of the Viking King would shatter the ladder.

Ki-Gor reached an adobe wall and vaulted over. He got a look as the King climbed off the ladder. Their eyes met for an instant. Ki-Gor saw only rage. He landed in a small courtyard, decorated with wooden carvings of ships and dragons. They looked very old.

The wall smashed in. Rock and mud bricks flew. Ki-Gor leaped over the wall on the other side of the private garden just as the home's owner emerged to discover the chaos in her own yard. She would have yelled in outrage, but saw the King's grim visage of fury. She ducked back into her house.

Ki-Gor was in the next yard. A stout broadsword and a circular shield leaned against the house. Ki-Gor grabbed the weapons and ducked around the corner of the house just as Bjärkamal smashed through the wall.

Ki-Gor raised his newfound shield and sword and waited with his back against the wall. Bodvär did not appear.

Freyrrun asked Helene, "How is it that you speak English?"

"My father taught me and many others. He had spent much time in a land he called Valhalla…"

Helene interrupted, "Isn't that the name of your heaven?"

Freyrrun shook her head. "This was a different Valhalla, one of wars and suffering, with wizards and dragons and horrible undead monsters. Father lived there for many years fighting in a war with many other soldiers. There were strange men and mechanical beasts. Father learned English from other Earthmen.

"Finally, he alone found a way to return home. But upon returning, he found his kingdom in ruins and all his family dead. He had been gone from Midgard nearly a hundred years. He gathered some willing men and women and set sail on a quest."

A crash up the street interrupted the tale. They ran toward it.

A tiny scuff of boot on rock alerted Ki-Gor. He whirled around and his shield took the hit from Bjärkamal. Had it not, he would have surely died.

As it was, Bodvär's mighty blow sent Ki-Gor flying over the front wall of the yard. He landed in a heap on the dusty street and slid toward the edge of the chasm.

His bare feet kicked at the smooth rock and Ki-Gor stopped himself just shy of the edge. A knotted climbing rope dangled behind him. A crowd had gathered to watch.

Ki-Gor eyed Bodvär as he pushed through the gate of the walled yard. The giant Viking had to duck under the gated arch. The homeowner peered out a second story window.

The King saw the Jungle Lord and accelerated. Ki-Gor threw his sword straight up in the air, grabbed the shield off his arm, and hurled it at the Viking King's head.

Without slowing, Bodvär raised his battle-hammer to block the shield. Metal clanged and sparked. Bjärkamal tore the shield in half, and the fragments slashed at the King's face, leaving a bloody trail.

Bodvär howled in rage and brought on the speed. The King figured to slam into the intruder and break his puny spine.

Ki-Gor plucked his falling sword out of the air and braced for impact.

Freyrrun and Helene pushed through the crowd just in time to see Bodvär bearing down on Ki-Gor. Helene screamed.

The Jungle Lord stood there while the King's rage propelled him like a charging rhino.

Just before the King reached him, Ki-Gor did a back flip off the ledge.

Bodvär's eyes shot wide open. He couldn't stop in time and charged off the ledge.

Freyrrun screamed, "Father!"

Giant fingers flailed and grabbed and finally caught the knotted rope. The Viking looked up and dodged. Ki-Gor's sword grazed the side of his head and slashed his shoulder, leaving a trail of crimson.

Ki-Gor was in his element. He certainly had no need for knots in the rope as he could climb vines like a monkey. The King followed, but Ki-Gor was much faster.

Freyrrun grabbed Helene's hand and ran. "Come on!" she said. Helene had little choice but to run. They raced along the ledge and approached the rectangular wooden tram. It started rising.

"Wait!" the Viking girl yelled. A flaxen haired woman looked out of the tram and it stopped moving. The two women ran in.

Inside the tram, there was a set of wooden gears and a crank. A pair of teenage boys stood at the crank.

Freyrrun urged them on, "Go! Go, go, go!"

They grabbed the crank and turned it rapidly. The wooden box moved upward.

Ki-Gor leaped from the rope to the edge of the tier above him. Bodvär wasn't far behind and soon reached the next tier -- the forth and upper-most level in the canyon. Ki-Gor's foot smashed into the King's face. The Viking held the rope with one hand and grabbed Ki-Gor's ankle with the other. Bodvär spat blood and sneered, "Not this time, intruder. Now you die!"

The King let go of the rope and grabbed Ki-Gor's legs with both mighty hands. The Jungle Lord's ankles were barely larger than the giant's thumbs.

Ki-Gor slid toward the edge, the weight of the Viking pulling him to-ward the brink. He teetered at the precipice and dug in his heels. Ki-Gor pounded the King's hands to no avail. He was slowly going over.

Inch by inch Ki-Gor's feet slid toward the chasm. Ki-Gor looked down and saw a pile of smashed lumber and rocks far below him. His toes were pulled over the edge.

The giant at the jungle man's feet started swinging.

A cabinet silently opened in an empty room. The Jackal peered out, sat-isfied that the room was unoccupied. The Jackal heard the battle between the Viking King and the Jungle Lord. Part of him hoped Ki-Gor survived. When the sounds of the fight moved outdoors, the Jackal decided it was time to make his move.

The fight distracted the occupants of the King's Public House. The Jack-al silently went to the front door and released Furcht and Schicksal. "Run!" he urged them. They took off.

Then, the Jackal moved toward the back wall and searched for anything out of the ordinary. It didn't take long to find something.

Opposite the main door, the Jackal saw a guarded opening, shrouded by a heavy leather curtain. A pair of stout Vikings stood in front of the curtain. They were armed with short handled hand-axes. The Jackal made sure they had not seen him watching them.

A woven divider separated the guarded space from a kitchen storage area. The Jackal found his way to this space without much difficulty. He had perfected his infiltration techniques during his training for the Reich

The giant at the jungle man's feet started swinging.

Arkanen Korps in the Great War.

A bucket of fish caught the Jackal's eye. He looked at the dead fish and the corners of his mouth curled up a little bit. He pulled a fish out of the wooden bucket and picked up a knife. He silently moved up to the screen that separated him from the guards and pressed the tip of the knife against the screening material. He hefted the dead fish in his hand.

One station over from the guards, a lone seamstress worked. She fashioned garments for the King and his family. She sat with an oversized pair of breeches in her lap and pulled the thread through, closing a seam.

A fish landed in lap. She screamed.

The guards looked at each other and ran off to check out the trouble.

The razor sharp knife glided through the fabric of the screen and the Jackal stepped through.

The heavy leather curtain was pushed aside and the Jackal slipped unseen into the cave. The mercenary flicked his lighter open and moved into the tunnel.

After a minute, the cave wall turned gently to the right. The air was cooler there.

His foot felt open air. He jerked it back and felt around. The Jackal found a pebble with his foot and nudged it off the edge. He counted. It took almost two seconds for the small stone to hit rock, so he knew the drop was about fifty feet.

In the distance he heard the leather curtain flap open and he saw a faint wedge of light.

"Get a torch, Erik," one of the guards said.

The Jackal quickly lowered himself off the edge and hung by his fingertips. He pulled himself up and looked down the passage at the opening. The leather curtain flapped open again and the Jackal ducked out of sight just as the guard carrying the torch entered.

The ceiling flickered faintly with torchlight. The Jackal saw it grow slowly brighter and heard boots crunch on the dirt floor of the cavern.

There was shouting outside the cave. The torch flew toward him and landed in a spray of dirt. The footsteps receded. The dim light flickered and revealed that he hung in a deep vertical shaft. Below his feet was a precipitous drop. He looked up. Off to the side was a ladder that led up into the darkness. Far above he felt, more than saw, a faint glow.

Silently, the Jackal moved hand over hand on the ledge until he reached the ladder. He scrambled onto the narrow ledge and started climbing. When he reached the thirtieth rung he felt the glow was growing stronger.

He counted eighty-seven rungs before he reached the summit. The drop to the floor of this vertical shaft approached two hundred feet. Above him the shaft disappeared in the darkness.

For the last twenty feet of the ascent, the Jackal made no sound at all. The glow grew stronger as he approached. But the light that came from the chamber was strange. It was not red or yellow, neither blue nor green or white. It was of no color and all color at the same time.

A numbing euphoria came over the hard-nosed mercenary as he reached the chamber. He eased his head up and peered into a circular cavern with a domed ceiling. Odd runes were carved into the rock on the ceiling and walls. There were no people there, but the room was far from empty.

Huge rectangular stone blocks stood in a circle. More stones lay in a horizontal circle across the tops of the vertical stones. The carved dome set atop this - or was the dome carved into the solid rock of the ceiling?

The Jackal climbed into the room and stared in amazement. A broad grin spread across his face. He had found something that had eluded explorers and adventurers for centuries.

In the center of the hengestones lay a beautiful pool. It was perfectly circular and shimmered with a beckoning, unearthly glow.

The Jackal sat down on an ornately carved stone bench and took off his boots.

The King's giant hand wrapped around Ki-Gor's leg like it was a twig. From the corner of his eye, Ki-Gor saw a strange contraption. It looked like a large wooden crate hanging from a stout rope. There were people inside. It was travelling fast; racing both up and across the cliff face.

From his years in the jungle, Ki-Gor had developed an unnatural sense of distance and timing. He saw that the wooden tram was going to pass below him and Bodvär by a score of feet. He decided landing on that was better than crashing on the rocks below.

The King of the Vikings, Bodvär the Bold pulled his face above the rocks. "I have you now, jungle savage," Bodvär sneered.

Ki-Gor snarled and said, "You may have me, but who has you?" He jumped. He pushed his mighty legs as hard as he could. Their bodies arched out away from the rocky ledge. Bodvär panicked and let go.

The pair flew through the air until they landed with a crash on top of the wooden tram. The force of their impact jarred one end of the rope cable loose from its fitting and the whole thing began to fall.

Inside the car, Helene and Freyrrun screamed. The other passengers panicked as well.

The thick rope raced through the iron and wood pulley on the roof of the tram. Ki-Gor grabbed it, but the line slid through his fingers and left a nasty rope burn. Bodvär reached over Ki-Gor's shoulder and grabbed the rope.

The crude elevator stopped with a lurch that nearly ripped the pulley out of its mooring. The passengers below were driven to their knees. The car swung wildly. Freyrrun slid toward the open side of the elevator car and floated in the air weightlessly. She drifted out of the wooden car.

Helene reached out and grabbed the Viking girl's wrist with one hand and a strap inside the car with the other. The car swung down and Helene pulled Freyrrun into the wooden car.

Bodvär hung on as the tram swung down and then back up again. Ki-Gor yelled, "Helene! When the swing reaches its highest point again, jump."

Helene watched the car swing up above the ledge and then down. As the car rose again, Helene pulled the scared Viking girl's arm and said, "Come on!" At the top of the swing they jumped and landed in a tangled heap on the massive rock ledge.

Bodvär let out some rope and the car careened toward the ground. Ki-Gor jumped and grabbed the line and started climbing up. The Viking King saw the smaller man getting away and cursed him.

The King was forced to lower the tram to the ground. When the passengers were safely down, Bodvär climbed the rope with wild fury.

With massive arms and unleashed rage, Bodvär chased Ki-Gor up the rope. Ki-Gor quickly scrambled all the way up to the mooring high above the uppermost level. He perched on a beam set into the rock. Cows and goats grazed in the fields below. In the distance he saw a small cemetery and stone circle.

Bodvär approached. Ki-Gor realized he had trapped himself. In his mad scramble away from the ferocious Viking King, he had gone too far up the line -- there was nothing but sheer rock above and an enraged Viking below. There was no way out.

Helene leaned out over the ledge and saw the tram on the rocks far below. Ki-Gor was nowhere to be seen. Her eyes followed the line up and saw the men high above.

Freyrrun looked from the climbing men to Helene and took her hand. "Come," she said and ran across the field toward the men. Helene took notice of a stone circle off to her right and was reminded of a childhood trip to the English countryside.

Ki-Gor pushed himself as far back on the mooring as he could. The stout rope looped through an iron ring attached to a huge beam that was sunk in the face of the rock wall. Ki-Gor locked eyes with the approaching Viking and unleashed a primal roar, one that had terrified many.

Bodvär grinned broadly, "You can not frighten me. I have fought winged demons on the volcanic plains of Valhalla. Battled legions of the undead. Faced magicks and sorcerers. I do not fear you." The giant pulled Bjärkamal off a hook on his belt and pointed it at the Jungle Lord. "Prepare to die."

Faint tendrils of energy snaked around the head of the battle-hammer like wisps of lightning. Ki-Gor had already witnessed the power the Hammer of the Gods could bring. He was as good as dead if he didn't act.

He dove off the mooring just as Bjärkamal's wrath smashed it behind him.

The mooring shifted in the cliff face and dropped a foot. Bodvär was jarred loose and clung to the thick rope with one hand. Ki-Gor leap sent him flying over the King. The Jungle Lord clawed frantically at the rope as he passed. The King swung the hammer wildly at Ki-Gor, but missed. The battle-hammer slipped from his grasp and plummeted to the pasture below.

Helene gasped when she saw Ki-Gor dive off the beam. The lightning crashed where her husband had been a moment before. Its thunder echoed through the canyon. Her husband slid down the tram's line and leaped the final twenty feet to the grassy pasture below. The soft grass cushioned his fall and he raced for the fallen hammer.

Helene and Freyrrun ran toward him.

Bodvär saw where Ki-Gor was headed and released his hand from the tram's cable. The Jungle Lord raced across the pasture. Bodvär landed with a tremendous shaking of the ground. He ran toward his fallen weapon.

Ki-Gor reached down to grab the battle-hammer at full speed. His finger's wrapped around the leather straps, but the hammer didn't budge, not an inch. Like it was glued to the spot.

Ki-Gor was flung to the ground by his own momentum. Bjärkamal did not move.

The King reached for the hammer with one hand and swatted Ki-Gor away with the other. The Jungle Lord went spinning into the grass. Bodvär the Bold picked up his battle-hammer and stalked toward the beaten jungle man.

Bodvär raised Bjärkamal and spat out, "Death is a but a mirror of a warrior's life. Fare thee well, jungle man. May you find peace in Valhalla."

The blue electric charge swirled around Bjärkamal's hammerhead. Ki-Gor staggered to his knees but was too dazed to turn away or run.

Helene's feet flew swiftly across the soft grass. She was headed directly at the Viking King. She saw the energy swirling around the hammerhead. She was going to be too late.

She made a sharp adjustment and instead of attacking Bodvär, she dove at her husband.

Bjärkamal sizzled with energy, the bolt of lightning suddenly exploded on a collision course with Ki-Gor. But Helene was a fraction of a second faster. She reached her husband just before the lightning did. The scintillating energy smashed into her instead of him and the fearless aviatrix was set aglow.

She flickered briefly with blue energy and then crashed to the ground a smoldering, lifeless husk; her chest a blackened cavity.

Ki-Gor screamed her name in horror and dropped to his knees beside his beloved bride. He cradled her lifeless face and looked into her eyes, once a brilliant blue, but now still. Dead. He screamed like a wounded animal. The misery tore at his heart. At that moment, he felt he had stopped living, too.

Freyrrun charged her father and pounded her fists against him. She got in a few good hits to the face before he slapped her to the ground. He stood for a moment and his gaze shifted from his sobbing daughter to Ki-Gor's desperate cries over the smoldering form of Helene. Bjärkamal slipped through his fingers and fell to the ground with thunderous finality.

Rage welled up in the Jungle Lord and pushed aside the grief. Ki-Gor turned to his attacker and the entire valley heard him roar in anguish. Bodvär was taken aback by the animalistic, primal ferocity of Ki-Gor's rage.

The King didn't move to avoid Ki-Gor's charge. The flying tackle hit Bodvär square in the chest and toppled him like a massive baobab tree felled by a thousand axes. Ki-Gor's fists struck blow after blow against the Viking's face.

The Viking girl regained her senses. She rolled over and crawled to Helene. Freyrrun pushed her hands beneath Helene's shoulders and lifted them up. Helene's head lolled back. Freyrrun dragged Helene across the grass.

After a minute, Ki-Gor stopped punching the unconscious king. He saw Freyrrun dragging his dead wife across the field and chased her down.

Ki-Gor yelled, "Stop!"

"We don't have much time," Freyrrun said calmly as she continued to drag Helene.

"Much time? She is dead."

Freyrrun brushed aside Ki-Gor's question and asked, "Are you going to help?"

Ki-Gor looked at her and then grabbed his wife and threw her limp corpse over his shoulder.

"Now what?" he said.

"Follow me."

Ki-Gor carried Helene across his shoulders. Freyrrun lead the Jungle Lord down a confusing series of ladders and passageways until they reached the King's Public House -- the longship's hull.

Ki-Gor stopped outside the building and said, "Why here? This is where all trouble started."

Freyrrun said, "Follow me, and stay close!" She pushed through the door. Ki-Gor trailed her reluctantly.

They approached the leather curtain and were blocked by the two guards. They said, "Halt!"

Freyrrun pushed past them and said, "Leave us alone Erik. There's no time for argument. And give me your torch."

She grabbed the torch out of his hands and threw back the curtain. Ki-Gor saw the cave beyond. Freyrrun marched in, the flaming torch lighting the way.

Voices echoed in the dark. The Jackal took a sip from his canteen and then plunged it into the shimmering pool. He pulled the canteen out and twisted on the cap. He slicked his wet hair back and grabbed his boots.

Freyrrun gestured with the torch. "Up there," she said.

Ki-Gor wondered how deep the cave was and why they were here. It seemed a waste of time. Were they headed to some Viking funeral ritual? He looked where the Viking girl was pointing and saw a ladder built into the rock face. It disappeared into the dark. A soft glow lit the ceiling of the cave far above.

Ki-Gor grabbed the ladder and climbed. Freyrrun followed with the torch.

Ki-Gor pushed Helene's body into the domed room and followed it in.

Freyrrun stepped into the chamber and walked to the pool's edge. She said gently, "Ki-Gor, bring her here."

Ki-Gor cradled Helene in his arms, looked at her lifeless face, and was glad he had closed her eyes. Emotion crept up on him in the dark. He cried soft, silent tears. They dripped down on his wife's face. He carried her over to the odd pool and laid her on the carved stone blocks that encircled the waters.

Letters ran in circles around the pool, but since Ki-Gor couldn't read, he had no idea that there wasn't a scholar in the world that would have been able read them either. They were impossibly ancient, and utterly otherworldly.

Freyrrun began singing in her native tongue. It was a song of heroes fallen and heroes snatched from the world, like her father, moments before their death in battle. She sang the song of the Våren Livet Farvann, a song she had sung only once before, but one that all the children of the village learned.

As she sang, a clatter came from the ladder. The Jungle Lord turned and saw the bloodied Viking King reach the chamber and climb in. Bodvär ducked his head under the archway at the entrance and removed his helmet. He looked down at Helene's body and sighed deeply.

Ki-Gor saw tears in the King's eyes as the enormous man sat quietly to the side.

The song meandered with words Ki-Gor did not understand, but he stayed silent. Freyrrun held a long note and reached behind a pillar for an ornate silver ladle. As she dipped the silver into the pool, her voice stopped.

The pool continued the song; the waters reverberated in sonorous tones as the illuminated fluid filled the well of the dipper. As it was lifted, the drops that escaped the well caressed the ladle and sang their return to the pool.

Freyrrun let drops spatter on the ancient writings. The glowing blue liquid welled in the crevasses of the sculpted runes. The ancient writing all around the pool glowed. The silver ladle reached Helene and Freyrrun let a precious few drops fall to her lifeless lips.

Ki-Gor looked up to Freyrrun. The girl smiled and said, "Yes."

He gently pushed Helene's chin with his thumb and parted her lips. Freyrrun tilted the ladle and the glowing water poured into Helene's mouth. Freyrrun returned the silver ladle to its hook on the pillar.

A warm glow started around Helene's lips and moved down her chest to where Bjärkamal's blast had ravaged her body. The glow swirled and brightened and then spread to all her limbs.

Ki-Gor backed away. He was nervous and afraid. He had never seen such magic. The glow strengthened and finally became blinding. At first, Ki-Gor shut his eyes, but he finally had to turn away and cover them with his arm. The light was too bright. Brighter than the sun.

How long the glow lingered and how long they were blinded after, they did not know. But in time, the room materialized out of the pure white that filled their vision.

Ki-Gor looked down at Helene, lying on the carved stones. Her leopard skin top was charred and blackened from the lightning strike, but as the glow receded from her body, Ki-Gor watched her flesh reform, the alabaster skin returned, unscarred and like new.

Helene gagged, forcing blood and water from her mouth. Ki-Gor dropped to his knees and cradled her head as she coughed up liquid. Then her eyes fluttered open and she took a sudden deep breath. She looked at her husband.

"Ki-Gor! Thank God you are alive!" she said. He kissed her deeply.

Her eyes took in the surroundings. She broke the kiss. "Where are we? What is this place?"

Bodvär stood and said, "You are in the sacred Våren Livet Farvann."

Freyrrun said, "You would say the Spring of Life Giving Waters."

Ki-Gor helped Helene sit on a stone bench. She looked at the arches, pillars, and the magnificent glowing pool and said, "This. This is what the Jackal was after. What he has been chasing all these years. The Fountain of Youth."

Bodvär kneeled before them. "'Tis more than that." He said, gesturing to the pool, "This is the Godt Våren, our greatest secret."

The giant of a man held out his hand to Helene and said, "Come, let us celebrate the correction of my most dire mistake. The waters have shown me what I could not see for myself. Your true nature was revealed when they shone a pure blue. And your selfless act that saved your husband? That tells me that he is pure of heart as well. Had the waters turned red, I would have had to kill you both on the spot."

The King clapped Ki-Gor on the shoulder; the force nearly knocked the jungle man to his knees. Bodvär roared, "But enough of that, now is the time for feasting!"

The Jackal waited until long after the sound of footsteps had left the chamber and trailed away down the ladder and out through the long cavern.

Five more minutes he forced himself to wait, unwilling to risk discovery. Then he edged around the corner and sneaked a look. The chamber was empty. He silently rose up on his feet and stepped over the stone bench.

As his feet tread on the carved runes that circled the pool he looked into its waters, searching for validation. A small swirl of red twisted up from the depths and broke the surface in the center of the pool. It was absorbed into the blue and tinted the water slightly violet.

The Jackal smirked and wondered how deep the pool was. But he wasn't willing to test it. He rested his hand on his full canteen and stepped out of the chamber.

Wooden plates jumped when the King pounded his empty stein to the table joyously. Helene jumped back a bit, but Ki-Gor was getting used to the massive fellow. The plates were heaped with crusty bread, braised antelope, and chopped green fruit. Helene wasted no time eating her fill.

Freyrrun sat next her father and seemed nervous. She picked her food apart, but ate very little.

Ki-Gor kept his eye on the King, and when thought the man was drunk enough, he leaned over to Bodvär and gestured up at the arched wood beams. He said, "How did you manage to get your ship all the way up here?"

The King laughed, "Well… That is the end of the tale, my lad. Quite a tale it is, too. Loss and redemption, and tragic loss again." He looked into his empty stein for a moment. "But here we are."

A maiden replaced his stein with a fresh one. The table was silent. Bodvär smiled at the girl as she left and took a draught of the thick mead. He said, "The tale, is it?"

"If you wouldn't mind," Helene said.

The King smiled. "Alright, then, for you. The tale of Bodvär the Bold is a strange and colorful one that starts long ago, when the Norsemen ruled the world. The Northlands were under attack by strange and powerful beings - creatures really - fleshy beasts that had no mind of their own, but when gathered in groups gained a kind of vicious intellect.

"They had made their way to my ancestral home, and were laying siege to my family's beautiful castle by the lake. Their awful weapons were collapsing the very walls of Castle Tarn.

"I grabbed Bjärkamal and my shield, and tore into the fray. Hundreds of the beasts fell, but finally their weapons of screaming horror shattered the very stone of the castle and it collapsed upon me. I was certain I would be crushed to death."

Ki-Gor and Helene looked at him and wondered how much of the tale was true, but after what they had seen in the Valley of the Lost, they were inclined to believe.

The King drained his mead and continued, "I blacked out. When I awoke I was with a few of my best warriors in a strange land. It was there that I learned of the Godt Våren, of their power.

"I learned that the same forces that brought down Castle Tarn had enslaved many worlds, including the new world I found myself in. In time, I joined with others warriors to fight the creatures. Some were from Midgard and some from other, far stranger worlds. Warriors from both the past and the future. Together we fought to keep the forces of darkness from reaching the Godt Våren of that new land. And finally, as I was dying in battle, I discovered a pool much like the one you have seen. I fell into it and was returned to Midgard to the very chamber you have seen. I was returned full health.

"The journey back to the fjords of the Northlands is a tale unto itself and perhaps I will regale you with it another day. Suffice it to say, that when I arrived home, there was little left. The horrid fleshy beasts had been defeated, but the castle and my lands lay in ruin. Nearly a century had passed since my departure."

Helene found her mind back at her days at Vassar. She remembered a European History class. "But that would have been more than eight hundred years ago."

Bodvär sighed, "Has it been that long? Odhinn, help me. Everything I knew was gone, so I recruited all who would join me to return here, to the Godt Våren of Midgard in hopes I could return to that other land. As you can see, we have lived here ever since, but the Godt Våren has never allowed a return trip to Valhalla."

"Shortly after returning here, our numbers rose rapidly, but the waters were depleted and could not sustain us. So we reluctantly had to limit the population of the village and could not permit any children. We kept our numbers strictly to that which the pool could sustain. This was a matter of life and death for the whole colony. The punishment for violating the trust of the community is death."

Helene caught Freyrrun's arched brow of concern. She looked at the young girl and nodded in understanding.

Freyrrun stood.

"Not now, daughter. Not now." She sat.

Bodvär looked at Ki-Gor and spoke in a serious voice, "As you can imagine, we cannot let outsiders partake of the sacred waters. I made an exception in the case of…"

"Helene. My wife."

"Your lovely wife. My daughter forced a correction of my mistake and in this case she was right. The waters do not lie. They clearly showed her honor and gallantry. And yours."

Ki-Gor smiled, "I do what I can to keep peace in my part of the world. To keep Bantu from killing Masai. To help the pygmy tribes from falling prey to the slavers."

Bodvär interrupted. "For that you should be commended. Tell me, Ki-Gor, can you walk away? Let us live in peace?"

The Jungle Lord nodded and said, "Provided that you take no actions against your daughter."

Freyrrun looked up hopefully.

Bodvär's lips inched up just a bit, like he wanted to smile, but resisted. His daughter had broken the rules and needed to suffer the consequences, as would anyone else. He said, "But she is an impetuous thing, and has broken our laws by leading you here." The King looked into his daughter's eyes. She glared back at him.

Helene interrupted, "She was running for a reason. You need to forgive her, whatever the reason. It is not her fault alone that we discovered this valley. There was also the Jackal. He is here somewhere and he is the dangerous one."

Bodvär nodded, "Of that you are right. Very well, you let us live in peace and I'll keep my daughter from exposing us to the world. I'll need to keep a better eye on her."

"Helene and I would never betray your trust, but that mercenary is another story. He will do what ever is best for him."

Freyrrun sobbed and Helene wrapped her arms around the girl. Helene said, "I understand. It'll be alright."

"Alright? How could this possibly turn out well? I have committed two or more violations of sacred law," the girl said. She turned and faced the King, "My father will have my head. He has to. It is his duty. It is said that he who cannot lead shall not. The people will rebel."

Helene said, "He would kill his own grand-child?"

Freyrrun burst into tears; her hands subconsciously touched her belly.

The Jackal stood at the edge of the jungle and looked down through the jagged precipice into the hidden canyon. Furcht whined at his side and he gave her neck a rub. Schicksal joined in and he patted both their heads.

He reached in a pocket and checked his compass. He rested his hand on his canteen a moment, and briefly wondered how long the water would last. It had only taken a ladle full to restore the jungle girl to full health. He would use the water sparingly. He knew he could never let the secret out. This was the edge he had been looking for. It would be a long trip back when he needed more.

The mercenary turned and looked at his hyenas as the sun neared the western horizon. "Time to go, girls, time to go. War is brewing and there's money to be made."

He walked away from the Valley of the Lost and stepped into the jungle.

"Father," the girl said, "I have broken one of the most sacred rules of the people."

"I forgive you for bringing these visitors to our land," the King said. He smiled at Ki-Gor and Helene and continued, "I feel they will become good friends of our people. But, you must not stray. Our secrets must be kept, for all our safety."

"That is not what I was speaking of, Father."

"Oh? Then what is this second transgression you speak of, my child?"

"That's it, Father. I am no longer a child, I am a woman now."

The King looked at her expectantly.

She took a deep breath. "I am a woman and you are to be a grand-father."

The King shot to his feet and shouted, "WHAT? Is this true?"

The girl looked down and whispered, "Yes, Father."

He glowered above her. Then the giant bent down on one knee. Even in that position he still towered over her. He put his finger under chin and lifted her face. She resisted, but finally looked into his eyes.

Bodvär smiled at her. "That's… that's wonderful. Wonderful!"

Freyrrun looked confused. "But it's forbidden."

"Not today, it's not. This week we lost twenty souls to the river god."

The young woman looked at her father and saw his full smile. Her eyes brightened and she leaped to her feet and threw her arms around her father's neck.

Ki-Gor had never seen a happier father and daughter in all his life. He looked at Helene and saw that she was watching Freyrrun with an odd expression. He searched for a word but his limited familiarity with the English language failed him.

Wistful, unfortunately, was not in his vocabulary.

THE END

Discovering the Other Jungle Lord

In my youth, I read Edgar Rice Burroughs, Lester Del Rey, Robert E. Howard, Doc Savage, The Shadow and other pulp series that I discovered in the local used book store. In the 1960s and 70s, publishers reprinted a lot of stories from the pulps.

After writing my Green Lama story, "The Studio Specter", Airship 27 editor Ron Fortier suggested I write either a Moon Man or Ki-Gor story. After looking into the characters, I decided on Ki-Gor because my Green Lama story was very urban, and I thought that delving into the heart of man versus nature would be a nice change.

However, before the writing, I had to do some reading. I had read a number of Tarzan novels in my youth, but I hadn't read any Ki-Gor. Despite my (false) assumption that the characters would be similar, I thought I had better read a Ki-Gor book or two before setting out. I first read two stories from later in the series that were reprinted in High Adventure Magazine. I liked them, but I really wanted to know more about how Ki-Gor and Helene met and fell in love. I picked up a reprint featuring the first two tales. Fortunately, many of the Ki-Gor novels are available in reprint form. What I found was that John Murray Reynolds had created a character and series that was really quite different than that of Tarzan, and one that I liked a lot. I ended up reading five Ki-Gor novels and a lot of material online before tackling my novella.

I came up with a series of short pitches for Airship 27, and Ron liked the Viking idea the best. Having written a few story fragments featuring a Viking named Bovar the Bold, I decided to include him in the story. I also wove in another original character of mine, the ruthless mercenary, The Jackal. When I got to the end, I knew my story went on far too long, so I tightened up the story and trimmed out a subplot featuring Ki-Gor's pygmy friend, N'Geesa. Now I had my tale.

I really enjoy the relationship between Helene Vaughn and Ki-Gor so I kept that at the heart of my story. What would *you* do for love?

W. PETER MILLER – is a film editor, author and blogger. He lives in Burbank, California with his three children. He enjoys playing volleyball and boardgames when he is not watching one of his children on stage in a choir or dance performance. You can find him online on Facebook, IMDB, and at www.docsavagetales.blogspot.com.

THE ALLURE OF THE JUNGLE

Of all the subgenres of the classic pulps, from westerns to crime and pirate stories, none were more popular to the fans than those set in the exotic jungles of the world. When one considers the globe of the 1930s, it is all too easy to understand the fascination these green swaths of landscape offered the imaginations of young pulp readers. From the moment Edgar Rice Burroughs first introduced the world to Tarzan of the Apes in the pages of *All Story Magazine,* readers were hooked with the locales in which these tales were set. Here was both primal beauty in the form of untainted virgin domains mixed with the raw savagery of Mother Nature's animal kingdom. It was a pure pulp blend that would keep fans enthralled for generations to come.

Jungle stories were as popular on film as they were in print, from pulps to comics. People of the era couldn't get enough of all those great characters from Tarzan, to Sheena, Ka-Zar, Tam, Son of the Lion, Jan of the Jungle, Sabu, Jungle Jim, and all their counterparts. Whereas the one stellar figure that easily outdistanced all the others and proved an admirable alternative to Burroughs Ape Man was the blond haired Ki-Gor, the Jungle Lord from the pages of JUNGLE STORIES.

Fiction House's JUNGLE STORIES began in 1939 and published 59 issues ending its run in the Spring of 1954. It featured gorgeous covers and interior illustrations. The Ki-Gor stories, most attributed to writers Stanley Mullins, Dan Cushman and Robert Turner all under the house name of John Peter Drummond were superior to most pulp thrillers and one of the reasons was their advanced moralistic approach to the black characters appearing in their tales.

Up until these stories, blacks had been relegated to racial stereotyping reflective of the era's blatant racism. There were no black heroic figures in pulp literature of the time. Which is why Ki-Gor's two closest allies, Tembu George and N'Geeso shone as an example of extraordinary editorial courage. Once called George Spelvin, Tembu George was an American, a one time Pullman porter and ship's cook, who jumped overboard in Mombassa and eventually became a powerful Masai chief. While N'Geeso was the four foot chief of the Kamazila Pygmy Tribe. Both were loyal to Ki-Gor and he always treated them as equals. They shared many of his adventures.

It was only a matter of time before we at Airship 27 Productions would have to do a jungle themed series. Initially, following the path of other recent reprint volumes and new original collections, we planned on giving Ki-Gor his own title because of his obvious popularity. But as we came closer and closer to assembling this first book, we began to understand that vast attraction of the jungle theme and realized limiting ourselves to one particular hero was the wrong track to follow.

Rather it seemed to make more sense to give the series a general title, much as the original JUNGLE STORIES that had featured Ki-Gor in the first place and not limit ourselves to just one character. That being the case, it is our hope that subsequent volumes of JUNGLE TALES will indeed focus on many of the dozens of truly unique and exciting jungle pulp heroes of old. Sure, Ki-Gor will return, he's too good a character not to. But we do hope to feature some of the more obscure jungle heroes as well with an occasional, lovely jungle queen peppered in among the mix. And who knows, maybe in a future volume, we'll do a big cross-over adventure wherein more than one classic jungle pulp hero will team with others in an all out jaunt to shake the very primeval forests in which they reside. If this is something you would like to see, please don't hesitate to let us know.

For now we hope you've enjoyed these three brand new Ki-Gor Jungle Lord adventures. We had a blast bringing them to you.

Ron Fortier
11 Aug. 2011
Fort Collins Co.
(www.Airship27.com)
(Airship27@comcast.net)

Airship 27

Coming from Airship 27 Summer 2012

Airship 27 Productions is thrilled to launch their latest pulp anthology—The Green Lama, Mystic Warrior.

Created by Kendal Foster Crossen back in 1940 for *Double Detective Magazine,* the character was intended to be competition for Street & Smith's *Shadow* title. When wealthy young socialite, Jethro Dumont, traveled to Tibet, it was in search of enlightenment and purpose for his life. These he found plus a very rare and unique talent for the mystic arts. Empowered by powerful, arcane abilities, he has set forth on a new and bolder path, one of truth and justice. With his Buddhist sensibilities, Jethro Dumont became the most unique and memorable pulp hero of them all, The Green Lama.

In order to protect his identity, Dumont created a second false persona, that of Buddhist Dr. Pali, Aided by young starlet Jean Farrell and Detective Carraway, The Green Lama thrilled readers young and old in both his pulp and comic book adventures.

Now he returns in new adventures written by today's action-adventure scribes. From the mountain tops of hidden Tibet to the streets of New York and the glitter of Hollywood, journey with this classic pulp icon as he once more battles the wicked in defense of the weak and innocent.

Jump aboard Airship 27 Production's newest pulp collection and get ready for old fashioned thrills.

PULP FICTION FOR A NEW GENERATION!

available Summer 2012 at
Amazon.com
and as a PDF file at
Airship27Hangar.com

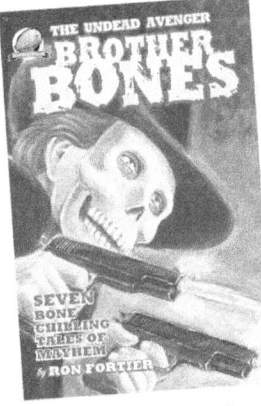